# POPCORN FOR BREAKFAST

I0539602

## JENNA GLEESPEN

Cover design by James Furlington

ISBN: 0615482325
ISBN-13: 978-0-615-48232-3

First Edition

# DEDICATION

To Dr. Paul Sirota,

For all your inspiration and guidance.

# POPCORN
# FOR
# BREAKFAST

Jenna Gleespen

# CHAPTER ONE

Laurie Bock stared at the glowing green numbers displayed on the sleek dashboard of her obviously expensive, yet not too overstated or flashy, luxury SUV. She slowly let out a slight sigh as her eyes shut and she leaned back into her warm, heated leather seats as traffic came to a dead halt. Exhausted and annoyed, she quickly reached for the glove box and pulled out a half smoked pack of Camel cigarettes.

She sat the smoke between her thin, painted lips and once again leaned back in effort to find any whim of relaxation as she lit the cigarette and rolled down her window. Again she sighed, but this time in relief as she once again shut her eyes and tried to ignore the blaring horns and cantankerous construction that surrounded her. She was almost oblivious to the long, routinely familiar, traffic ridden drive home from the office. That was until that sing-song, classic ringtone blared through the car speakers thereby breaking the short silence. Laurie glanced at the name on the telephone screen. DAVE NOVELL, it read. It was her boss. She quickly slammed the button on her sleek, new, trendy fad gadget next to her, threw out her quarter smoked cigarette, cleared her throat, rolled up the window, and answered in a short and professional tone, "This is Laurie."

"Laurie, good news. We loved your article on that writer you covered, eh what's his name?" The voice on the other end blared.

"James Bennet," she cut in.

"Ah yes, James Bennet, right, right. Well either way, it was brilliant. Bill wants you to be our new feature writer for page six. Don is gone as of next week and, well kid, you've got what the people want to hear, what they want to know. You up for it?"

"Well, Dave, that's just fantastic. Of course. Of course I'm up for it! So what happened with Don?"

"Oh never mind Don, he's not covering entertainment and arts anymore. He's moved on I suppose. Ha. But that doesn't matter neither way. We want you. "

*Either* she thought. *It's either.*

"Yes, yes, of course I'll do it. Thank you Dave. Oh my God, you know how long I have been waiting for this? Dave you are ama…"

"Good. Good. Your first story will be due the 25$^{th}$. That's roughly a week and a half. I'll call you in the morning to discuss the details. You can come in Thursday and sign that necessary paperwork bullshit. Told ya to stick with the Seattle Tribune, kid."

"Again, I don't know what to say…"

"Don't say anything kid, just go and celebrate. Take tomorrow off. I'll call you by 10 am. Gotta run. "

*Click.*

"Thank you Da...," she once again blurted as she realized that he had already gotten off the line.

She smiled, threw her head back, her hands up and slammed her bony finger tips down upon the steering wheel as she squealed, "Yes!" She reached again for the glove box and pulled out the pack of half smoked Camel cigarettes as she lit one with a smile that couldn't seem to fade away.

Laurie Bock had been working for The Tribune for nearly three years and had dreamed of her chance to be a feature reporter since her days at Stanford studying Journalism. Or so she had convinced herself. In all reality she had dreamed of the glamour and rouse as a big time Hollywood entertainment reporter in Los Angeles. But as time went by, expenses went up and job prospects went down, she decided to settle for a smaller market and grace the pages of The Seattle Tribune. Thus, reporting on much less exciting affairs than the latest rampages of California socialites, party girls, and cadaverous, rich little assholes.

Now there she was, a feature reporter in Seattle, Washington. Not what she had originally set out for, yet still a prideful career that instilled her with her own self-involved sense of satisfaction and the fat paycheck provided for her by the self-righteous editor at Seattle's number one selling newspaper.

Once she was in her uptown, ritzy, far too overpriced condo she showered, ordered in and slipped into a chic, short, gray, slinky dress. Again that aggravatingly familiar classic tone of the cell phone company echoed against the cathedral ceilings and high walls of her apartment home. This time she answered in a short, but sweet voice, "Hi, Tom."

"Hey, doll," the voice echoed back through the earpiece.

"And what is it that you could be calling for this evening?" She replied in a sensual voice that was noticeably infused with a hint of laughter.

"Ah, how about dinner? Or no dinner. Doesn't really matter either way I suppose." He spoke softly and in a slow pace that insinuated all the notions of a deep-seeded, passionate romance.

But Laurie knew that familiar tone of Tom's voice. It was not the tone of deep-seeded, passionate romance but more of a subtle hint at an attempt for a late night, lustful encounter.

"I simply don't have the time right now," she responded, "perhaps later. Goodbye now."

*Click.*

And that was Tom. A quick but constant pick-up followed by the same sudden goodbye. Ironically enough it was what Tom wanted with all the women he had encountered. It was what she was to him at first too. Laurie was nothing but a quickly picked up lay and an even quicker part. But he found himself head over heels for her and far too proud too admit that his promiscuity had wandered a little farther than his heart could handle. She smiled and laughed as she shook her head full of strategically placed, over-dyed hair and grabbed her lower-end designer handbag and locked her door as she set out toward her favorite uptown bar.

– – –

Laurie was an attractive girl. A thirty something, medium height, noticeably tanned over pale skinned woman with a jaunty face that was reminiscent of a wannabe supermodel that had just missed the cut. She knew the power of her sex appeal, and by God, did she use it. She was determined to get the attention of any man she desired and then in the change of a wind gust, blow him off, shoot him down or just plain use and then abuse him. A symbol of change in typical, revolutionary, feminist America, Laurie stood for what women resented in all men. What they so craved to embody yet never could admit they wanted. She was their poster child, their spokesmodel. She spoke for all the women that day dreamed of passionate fantasies that swept them off their department store heels and made them feel on top of the world as they lived vicariously through risqué, meaningless encounters.

She was powerful. She was beautiful, promiscuous, intriguing. She got what she wanted and kept complete control. All her affairs, despite the pseudo confidence they instilled in her, were kept secret, however. The don't ask, don't tell policy strictly applied to Laurie's love life. While she was not at all ashamed of her promiscuity, she was surely not outright with her sexual endeavors. Keeping a distance from people and emotions was maintaining a powerful persona that never could be hurt or belittled in Laurie's eyes. She made certain to never let people in too far and was proud of the detachment. For Laurie, sex was just that, a way to detach. It was power to her. The power she had always wanted. It was the power, the glamour, the rouse and the excitement of the fabulous tabloid lives back in LA she had become so blindly consumed by.

— — —

By two O'Clock in the morning Laurie was lying listlessly intoxicated in her uncommonly soft and pillow-laden bed. As she lay there she thought of the men she had briefly met at that posh little uptown bar she so often frequented. She thought of the bartender, Jimmy, that had had her once and ever since tried eagerly to have her once more as he poured her premium liquor martinis and flirted charmingly with her, feeding her booze and the all too familiar, heard once too many times pick up lines. She giggled, quietly to herself, as she thought of the poor horny souls she could oh so easily have had and that wanted her just too much for her to take any particular interest. She giggled as she thought of the men that thought of themselves as the suave ones, the ones that could grace a room with their pompous, daring little charm and take home any innocent victim they desired. She giggled some more as her subconscious boastingly told her, "Yeah, babe, you showed them all."

Then she pictured Tom, lying there next to her in passion that had been blinded by pride and ego. She lay there, still, smiling as she drunkenly reached for her trendy little phone, paged through the address book until the cursor landed upon the entry named TOM MOORE. She pressed the send button, let it ring twice, hung up and turned her phone off before setting it upon the night table next to her. Laurie lay there and once again thought about the men in her life. She could have dialed so many of their numbers to have them there in an instant. Yet her phone was now off and she rolled to her back, turned out her lamp, dragged her hands across her slim, toned, naked stomach and felt the emptiness inside.

Laurie waited anxiously for a call from her boss as she sat and watched the ten O'Clock morning news with her bottle of water that was sworn to come from the best springs on the face of the planet. She really loved Coca-Cola, but gave it up years ago and began drinking the well-marketed bottled waters in pursuit of a thinner waist line and a health-trendy lifestyle. Once she had gotten her fill of the shocking stories about morally bankrupt criminals, murderers and scandalous political affairs, she changed the channel to another station that thrilled her with a completely different form of brainwashing. It was an entertainment channel. Intellectually devoid, utterly pointless stories about idolized celebrities who's lives seemed so much more interesting to become involved with than the actually meaningful events that take place behind the backs of people just like Laurie Bock. As she stared at the television set she became just another mindless sucker that had been reeled into a false sense of security by believing that the beautiful people she saw on TV had it all and set an achievable standard.

Only that standard was not at all achievable by those who reveled in it. In fact, that desired standard that had been set was nothing but a lesser goal that had, for some reason, become important in most of society's eyes. And all those miserable beings that discovered intellect and truth over so-called normality and acceptance knew it. As much as Laurie knew that deep down, as much as a long lost part of her past had begged to remind her, she forgot it and became devoutly consumed by all the bullshit spat at her by the greedy media moguls of her world today.

Then, there it was. The sound she had been waiting for. She grabbed the phone off the arm of the couch and after clearing her throat, answered, "Hello, this is Laurie."

"Laurie," the short and tense voice replied. "The story you'll be covering for your upcoming feature is going to be on an author and motivational speaker that will be visiting Seattle this Saturday."

She listened eagerly to Dave's voice.

"Ok. Well we're interested in this story cuz this guy is sweeping the country with his tours, really giving it to people how it is, telling them how to live successfully, but not in that better your life in three easy steps kinda a way either. This guy's pretty interesting. People are eating him up. Make it good."

Laurie was already jumping to get started. She was desperately ready to get started on her first feature story and her feature career that she was sure would only catapult her success to a higher level.

"Ok. Ok. So what is his name? I'll start researching him right away."

"Jack Foster," said the voice.

She was silent for a moment. She gulped, took a breath and said, "Yeah. Sounds…" She cleared her throat. "Sounds great, Dave. I'm already on it."

*Fuck*, she thought as she got of the line. *Fuck.*

# CHAPTER TWO

Jack Foster was a silhouette of Laurie's past that was purposefully lost and utterly disregarded by none other than Laurie herself. They had dated in college. Back at Stanford University, in a time that now seemed like a faded dream or drunken memory they had more than dated. Laurie and Jack were in love. Or at least what Laurie considered love before she fell victim to the world around her. What most young, naïve, carefree, fun-loving souls who care nothing about the wicked ways of the world and are intent on achieving a much more romanticized version of life consider love. Jack and Laurie were young then however and unaware of the ways that the world could easily mold and change them. Unaware that they would make a choice to either let the molds cast around them or run and savor every bit of their individuality and true character. They were also unaware that those changes that the world would force upon them could possibly dictate their love for each other and wash away the passion and joy that they shared. They once believed in innocent, pure, fantastical love. The two were nearly inseparable. They shared the same ideals, the same philosophies about life, the same desires, wants and needs. It seemed as if at one time they honestly believed that the world was not capable of hardening them so much as to rip away their affection for each other and transform their love into nothing more than a drunken memory or faded dream.

Since her days at Stanford, Laurie, like so many others, had changed. Laurie once embraced a sort of rebellion and strong sense of freedom. She lived carelessly and without any real direction. Money was no object to her. Success was not important. The affairs of America's sweethearts and the latest and greatest materialistic desires in the world meant nothing to her. Soon enough, however, Laurie was consumed by the stresses and worries of the real world and decided to take the path that seemed so certain to make all her uncertainties and woes dissolve away.

Jack was just as carefree, spontaneous and rebellious as Laurie. He cared nothing about what anyone thought. Not his peers, not his parents, his friends and certainly not society. He laughed in the faces of those who held jobs that they despised, worked for people that they hated and used money as an excuse to keep at it. Jack once hated money. He thought it was useless and pointless. Long ago, back at Stanford, Jack swore that he would never crave, want or work needlessly for money.

Right around that time Laurie walked away from Jack. In her eyes, he was going no where; he had no desire to get a reputable job and earn a stable living. At least he refused to get what Laurie considered to be such. He blatantly refused to do that. He said he could make money his own way, be fine and stay happy. The problems and worries that plagued Laurie seemed secondary to Jack's fear of living life on someone else's terms. So they said goodbye and searched for their own meanings of success and happiness.

Laurie went on to pursue of a more materialistic and traditional sense of security while Jack decided to make his own rules and live life freely and vicariously in a real fly by the seat of your pants kind of fashion. Jack was smart. He capitalized on his apathy for what so many morons in the world today considered to be success. He threw it back in everyone's face that they had been consumed by the false hopes of the world around them. He wrote books, he freelanced; he gave speeches and even did standup comedy. And now he was a renowned author and motivational speaker that those same saps, the ones that had clung onto their neighbor's dreams and expectations for so long, had come to rave about. Just like Dave Novell said to Laurie in that phone call only moments ago: they were eating him up. He found it truly ironic that those poor idiots would spend their time and money to come see *him* and go out and buy *his* books just because a bestselling metropolitan newspaper or top ranked TV show had told them to. Jack gave it to people straight. He told them they were wrong, that they had been tricked. He told them that their lives had become utterly meaningless because they blindly followed some other asshole's idea of contentment and success. He tried to make people understand that they could work for themselves instead of for some greedy corporation. He told them they could make their own schedules, answer to only themselves and really start enjoying their quickly fading existence.

Most of Jack's fans would try out his philosophies, too. They would attempt to live a life free from absolute control and strict conditioning. They would sometimes quit their jobs, try to write a novel, start their own work-from-home business or attempt to be original in some way that allowed them to revel in laziness and truly have fun with their pathetic lives. Alas, when their creativity and inspiration would falter and those oh so familiar worries and fears resurfaced, they would quickly jump back onto the path that they had been pressured to follow their entire lives.

Now Laurie was covering Jack Foster. Feelings, thoughts and memories suddenly struck her head on and forced her to remember Jack. For a moment she sat on the sofa, phone in hand, and helplessly let so many emotions that had for so long seemed absent wash over her and drown her in their memory.

*Fuck*, she thought. *Fuck.*

The moment she hung up the phone she wished so much to pick it back up, call her boss, refuse to cover the story and if it had to be so even quit her job working for The Tribune. She wanted to run. She wanted to run away from it all. Jack Foster was a part of her past that she tried so steadfastly to discard, hide and forget once and for all. As she stood there and the reality of what had come smacked her in the face, she realized she had to come to terms with what was about to happen. She was about to be face to face with Jack Foster again. He was, after all, the only man she had honestly loved and had perhaps shown her, if at least for only a second, how life should really be lived.

It scared her. She knew the man that Jack once was and she knew he hadn't changed much. So far as she knew he was still that same egotistical, lazy, carefree and fancy- laden punk that she had fallen so helplessly for. And he was. Only Jack had grown up quite a bit, and too, started to learn the trade of the real world. That was exactly what infuriated Laurie the most. It was the fact that she had cashed in her innocent, fun loving persona for a perfect little job, a fancy car and a far too overpriced condo in the city while he simply had not. And yet, he had it all. It struck her there and then, he was right all along. She was, after all, covering *him*. People wanted to see him. People wanted to hear about him. Her first feature story would not be on some high listed, Oscar winning celebrity that she had dreamed of quoting, but on a mere vision of her past. A vision that now filled her with frustration, confusion and emptiness as she tried to reassure herself that her personal life would not get in the way of her work or her money.

What angered her most was that she had worked so hard. She had done everything right, or so she thought. That was before this unexpected glimpse into her past stripped her of her self righteousness and tore down her confidence and pride. *No way*, she thought. *No way will I let this asshole get to me.*

So she went into the kitchen. She pulled out the dry gin, the vodka and the vermouth and proceeded to make herself a martini breakfast.

By noon Laurie had really began to delve into the dilemma before her. She sat on her plush sofa tragically swinging her Martini glass back and forth as she thought of subtle insulting phrases that she would spit at Jack. Laurie started to drift off into a vindictive train off thought. *Who said my story had to idolize him? Who said it couldn't rip him apart, tear him down, and show the world what a pathetic fraud he is?* She smiled as these thoughts ran through her mind and she took another sip of her third martini for that day.

— — —

On the southern coast of Florida, in a posh suburb of Miami, Jack lie sprawled out on a bed sans clothing. The bed was soft. He sunk right in to the silky white sheets and slowly turned his head as he struggled to wake himself. As he opened his eyes and saw long, blonde curls inches away from him he quickly realized the bed he was laying so comfortably in was not his own.

*So who's?* He thought. Jack surely had no recollection of the current boudoir setting or of the mane of luscious locks that laid before him. He grinned and stretched his hands over his head, smiled as he looked over at the nameless sleeping beauty next to him and stumbled to find his clothing before heading for the door. It was three O'Clock in the afternoon when Jack arrived back at his home. He opened the cabinet above the sink and reached for the bottle of malt whiskey that sat in front. He eyed the liquor from the bottom of the bottle before opening it, taking a swig, then pouring the remainder into a glass that had been sitting on the counter. The warm relief of booze trickled down his throat as he turned around and glanced at his half filled in calendar, realizing that he had a flight to Seattle the next day.

"What the hell is in Seattle?" he asked his agent over the phone.

"The start of your tour, Jack. What do you mean what the hell is in Seattle?" the voice bellowed.

Laughing, he said back, "I know. I know. I'm simply joking, Stan. I'm all ready to go."

"Yeah? Really? Are you?" Stan asked.

"Well, I'll be ready. Give me ten minutes. I'll be packed and out the door," he said in a voice camouflaged in laughter.

"Jack, put the goddamn drink down and pay attention. This is your career. I haven't busted my ass for you to take everything laid out before you for granted."

Laughing once more Jack uttered, "No of course you haven't, Stan. You've busted your ass for me to get that sweet little Boxster you've been zipping around in." His laughter continued and warded off any attempt at a serious conversation that Stan had made.

"Be on the plane, Jack. I mean it," Stan ordered.

As Jack hung the phone up he propped himself on the countertop, nodded his head slowly to himself, leaned back to his elbows and swallowed the remaining whiskey in his glass. As much as Jack hated having Stan as an agent, as much as Jack hated the idea of even having an agent, he dealt with it and kindly employed his little brother.

It was quite ironic that Stan had become so consumed with Jack and his success. It was oddly ironic that Stan now catered to Jack, supplied him with opportunities and helped him achieve his dream lifestyle that he was living today. At one time Stan looked down upon his older brother. Although he perhaps should have looked to Jack for guidance and advice he instead despised him and even resented having any relation to his own kin.

But, Jack had proved Stan wrong, just like he had so many others. So Stan was now working for Jack. He was his agent. He guided Jack's career and helped Jack fulfill his dream of a life of pure contentment all for the sweet cash flow of brotherly love that Jack so generously provided.

Stan had at one time aspired to be an investment banker. He had first heard the words from his father. Looking back he could remember his deep, stern voice saying, "You don't want to be a teacher, son. There's no money in that. How about an investment banker? Ever think of that, Stan? That's a career that will really fill your pockets." But at the age of nine, Stan had no idea what an investment banker was. At that point his career options had been limited to that of a fire-fighter, a teacher, a doctor, lawyer, veterinarian or something equally as boring that laid along the lines of societal mediocrity. From that point on Stan realized that work was not about love, it was about money. Although he had no earthly idea of what the job of an investment banker entailed, he eagerly changed his career path and focused on the green. After all, money would ultimately make him happy, or so he had been trained to believe. His father had tried so steadfastly to instill in him, and in Jack for that matter, the idea that money was success and hard work was the only way to achieve it.

Stan listened while Jack did not. Stan adhered to his father's preaching, his lectures and his advice. He followed his word and focused on a career that he so believed he could really bank on. In the end, Stan was wrong. As was his father. The market slumped, luck went down and Stan slowly lost interest and money alike. All the while Jack had not a care in the world. He was just as broke as his brother, only also unemployed, lazy and drunk. Stan could not understand how Jack could possibly be happy. He was jealous although he would never admit that to anyone or to himself. Jack was unaffected by the woes of the world and convinced that money was simply society's false Messiah. So he did what he believed to be easiest; he wrote a book. He strung together a slew of drunken thoughts, mindless babble and intermittent sleazy sex scenes that soon transpired into a best selling New York Times novel. Stan lived off of the rest of his savings while Jack completed his lousy little work of fiction and sold it for a nice chunk of change. Of course, Stan was flabbergasted. He couldn't comprehend the idea that he had worked so hard, put so much at stake and cared just a little too much while Jack simply had lain on his ass, spat out ramblings from his drunken mind, and somehow managed to make the money that Stan had always dreamed of.

The next evening Jack had already arrived in Seattle and was sitting at the hotel bar. He had his whiskey glass in hand as he flirted shamelessly with the red-head seated next to him.

# CHAPTER THREE

Laurie waited anxiously for Saturday afternoon to arrive as her bedroom alarm clock struck four in the morning. She thought intensely about a past life shared with Jack as she wondered how her emotions of anger, pride and absolute fear would mix peacefully and possibly warrant an attempt at a respectful meeting. It seemed as if it could not be so. None the less, Laurie swore to herself that she would uphold the morals of a strict professional and not allow a ghost of her younger years to threaten anything that she had built for herself today.

For once in many years Laurie questioned herself. She felt inadequate to Jack, even though at one time she had believed that she was of higher stature, that she deserved better, could do better and should have more. Now she felt that Jack had the final laugh. She had no idea how to deal with the fact that she had left him only for him to prove her wrong in the end. She thought to herself, *How could he possibly have gotten this far? He was a loser, a slack-off, a joke. How did he end up better off than me?* Those thoughts haunted Laurie. At four a.m. on that Saturday morning Laurie swore that she would put an end to Jack's carefree ways.

As she drove to the convention center she pulled her second cigarette for that morning out of the half-smoked pack of Camels patiently waiting for her in the glove box. Not a word of what she would say to Jack had been rehearsed. Laurie wanted to keep it that way. So when the familiar questions reporters like her were trained to ask would boil in her head, she would inhale the rich tobacco quicker and raise the volume on the car stereo. Still Laurie's thoughts bellowed over the voice of the 80's rock vocalist blaring through the speakers. Flustered and annoyed with her inability to change her train of thought, Laurie jerked her steering wheel to the left and pulled up to a gas station. There she turned her car off. With elbows on the steering wheel she brought her hands to her face, closed her eyes and sighed. Picking her head up, shaking it remotely as if to clear the voices running wild through her mind, she took a breath and grabbed the bottle of Xanex out of her oversized, designer bag. Popping one she breathed in deeply once more, cleared her throat, started the car and headed to the convention center, a little more at ease.

In the truth of the matter, Laurie did not really have an anxiety disorder. In fact, she carried no disease that would possibly require the aid of such a drug. She, of course, felt differently about the subject. If anyone asked her she would swear that she was a constant sufferer of immense anxiety, often caused by stress, which leads her to drinking, which in turn only heightens her anxiety and deems her life ultimately uncontrollable without the help of pharmaceuticals. If prescription drugs like Xanex had not been considered trendy by those fools who believed life was just too hard to deal with, Laurie certainly would have never even scheduled the appointment to get them in the first place.

It was her co-worker Stephanie who first planted the idea in her head. Noticing how Stephanie graced the office with a relaxed confidence gained Laurie's attention and through subtle prodding she got her to spill the secret.

"Oh, they're great!" She can remember tall, skinny Stephanie saying. "I used to get so worked up over the littlest things, and now, what would you know, I could handle a million and one things at once if they were thrown my way." With that Stephanie slipped Laurie the phone number of a doctor as she winked and put her hand around her shoulder as if to tell her acquaintance that everything was going to be okay.

Laurie walked out of that doctor's office truly believing that she was a victim of a severe anxiety disorder and relieved that she was now cured of her oh so horrible stresses and woes. Now there she was, three years later, popping the same little pills to deal with the worries and problems in life that just never seemed to go away.

As she entered the convention center, pride and ego steadfast in hand, she walked to the back corridor and turned down a hallway to see Jack standing there. He was tall, lean and jovial. He was stroking some red headed girl's hair before she giggled, hugged him and walked away. Laurie had her eyes focused straight on Jack's face. It was aged but still as she remembered it. His pale complexion highlighted his intense blue eyes and his lips formed an amiable smile that seemed glued to his face in a cock-eyed slant.

He looked up and saw Laurie. She cleared her throat and walked towards him as she put her hand out and in a deep strong voice said the word "Jack" before frustratingly shutting her eyes and correcting herself. "I mean, Mr. Foster…"

He stopped her right there. "What?" he squealed as his smile straightened out and the corners of his lips almost touched the bottom of his eyes. "Mr. Foster?" He laughed, ran over and put his arms all the way around Laurie before she could speak another word. He lifted her off the floor for a moment, set her back down and put his hands on the sides of her face. She immediately pulled away as she straightened out her white suit and attempted to hide her quiet smile.

"Would ya look at you," he said. "Miss big time news reporter. It is still miss isn't it? You didn't run off and get married on me did ya?"

"No," she replied as she straightened out her knee-length skirt. "I believe we have a story to do."

"Well I'll be damned. I never would have believed it had I been told. Laurie Dreusel, here to write a story on me."

"Right. Well its Laurie Bock now. I had my name changed. Its been a long time, Jack, and I think we should just handle this whole thing professionally."

"Bock?" His laughter rolled through the air, "and where'd ya come up with that one? And why'd ya even change it in the first place you crazy girl?"

"It looked better in print," she replied stoically. "Now can we get on with this? I just have a few questions to ask you before I watch your speech or whatever you call it so I can write this feature and get on with the week."

Jack stood there stunned. For once the man of a thousand words had nothing to say. Not even the mist of a thought traipsed through his mind as he heard her request echoing loud and clear.

"Laurie," he said. His eyes saddened and his simpleton smile fell from his face. "What? What's the matter?

It's good too see you. I mean, I would have thought, would have hoped you would feel the same way."

She thought about what to say for a moment before softening her harsh voice and uttering, "I'm sorry. It's just, you know, it has been a long time. I, I don't really know what else to say."

"Of course," he replied as that amiable smile formed again on his face. "Well, relax lady, it's only me."

She smiled and nodded in agreement, a bit embarrassed that she had acted so brazenly.

"Step into my office," he joked, pushing open a door to a room with a desk, mirror, sofa and two chairs.

They both sat on the leather love-seat as he softened the tension with a friendly game of catch up. Laurie was at ease. Perhaps it was the Xanex but the rock hard façade that she had walked into that building with crumbled into a million pieces as Jack chiseled away to uncover the old Laurie, trapped deep inside.

# CHAPTER FOUR

All the information Laurie needed for her feature had been collected as the seminar came to an end. She had planned to meet Jack back in that same room in the back corridor after his lecture. Jack, of course had asked her to as they walked out of the room moments before he was to go on stage. She quickly accepted without any reluctance. But as the hazy fog that had settled as a result of the Xanex and martini she had earlier that day wore off, she bolted for the door as soon as Jack's body slid behind the curtain after waving goodbye to the crowd.

In the back room Jack explained to a lovely red-head that something came up and he simply had to be on his way. Promising he would be in contact with her before his departure from Seattle, he kissed her goodbye in a way that whispered "so long forever." It was pretty typical of Jack to do such a thing. Of course, he always displayed the behavior of a true gentleman while with the poor girls, only soon after would forget them and be on to the next, somehow never making them feel forgotten even though he never called. Laurie was an exception however, she always had been. He waited for her to come through the door, but as two hours passed and he realized she wasn't coming he went back to his hotel room to meet up with his glass of whiskey.

The next morning Laurie's phone rang. She didn't recognize the number. She answered and was surprised to hear Jack's voice on the other end.

"How did you get my number?" She asked without hesitation.

Laughing, he replied, "Easy, your editor gave it to me. I told him I needed to get in touch with you for this story. You didn't really think you could just run away from me now did you?"

"That had been the plan, Jack," she said in a tone soaked in irritation.

"Ah, I see how it is. I guess little Miss, what is it again, Bock? Well I guess she's just too good to have a nice evening with an old friend."

"Jack, it's not that, it's just that this is business," she explained.

"Psh, the hell with business. Meet me for lunch." His voice was eager and jovial, just as she would expect it to be. Even though she had stood him up the day before, Jack's spirit had not been walked upon and he persisted with a lovable cockiness that was evident in all that he did.

"Jack, I can't. I have things to do. I'll email you the story, it will be out this coming Thursday." With that, she hung up the phone.

Of course, Jack had tried to call back Laurie throughout the day, leaving messages of banter on her voicemail. She refused to pick up. The fear that he could possibly force her to rediscover her long lost self threatened all that she knew and strived for today. That fear paralyzed Laurie. It kept her from continuing a passion filled friendship years ago and now kept her from having a simple lunch with an old friend.

So Jack flew out of Seattle the next morning after waking up to the familiar vagueness of what had occurred the night before and a head of full, flowing hair lying next to him. That same morning Laurie had turned in her first feature story and gotten an overwhelmingly positive review from her pompous editor by four p.m.

The story did not necessarily tear Jack apart as she had contemplated doing. It did not expose him to be a selfish, carefree slacker who had gotten to where he was from luck alone. The feature did, however, hint that Jack was a bit of a playboy who lacked hard work ethic and maturity. Not so oddly enough, people were enthralled. They loved Jack. To them he was a modern day super-hero who had swooped in with well to do knowledge that was sure to change the way society would look at money and success.

The week after the story was printed Laurie was summoned into her editor's office.

"Well, kid, you know the story was a hit, not too shabby, but I've told you this already so I didn't call you in to kiss your ass," the white-haired, leather-skinned, wrinkled man sitting behind the mahogany desk said.

"Right, glad you liked it," she politely replied.

"Ok, so we need a follow up. This time, focus on the personal life of this Jack Foster. I think people will still want more. They'll want to know who he is. Put something together kid, have it to me by next Monday, that'll be your feature for next week," he ordered.

"Sure, no problem. But, is Mr. Foster still even in town?"

Laurie wanted the answer to be no. As difficult as it was for her to shield off Jack, it was far more devastating for her to admit that she had become just another media fed subhuman searching aimlessly for its next meal. Back at the convention center, Laurie could feel Jack peeling away every layer of her that had accumulated over the past five years. She hated that. She hated that and she hated that Jack had the power to make her realize her life was becoming more vague and obsolete as her years proceeded forward.

"Hell if I know kid, you're the reporter, use some of those skills you learned in college and track this guy down. Interview him over the phone for all I care, just get the juice and get it to me."

A phone interview didn't seem nearly as intimidating. Right then, with that thought Laurie came to understand that she was utterly intimidated by the person she tried so devoutly to write off.

"Ok Dave, I'll get on it."

As Laurie walked back to her desk she cursed under her breath as she wondered how the hell these odds possibly came up, surely not in her favor. Once she was in her swivel chair, she paged through her phone to find the number that Jack had called her from last week. She dialed it and waited for Jack's voice.

"Jack, its Laurie. Look, I need to write another feature on you," she blurted out hastily.

"Oh, well I guess I'm pretty popular then huh, or was this just all your idea?" he joked.

"No, Jack, my editor wants another story. This time he wants it to be more about your personal life and what not. We can do an interview over the phone. If you have time now, that would be great, if not then we can schedule a different time."

"Nonsense, you crazy girl. I'll come straight to you. I'm in Denver now, I have a seminar tomorrow but I think it can wait. I'll be in Seattle by tomorrow night. Oops, gotta run!" He hung up the phone before Laurie had the chance to decline his imposition. He had meant to do this and in all reality he did not have to run anywhere. Slyly and with selfish intentions conjured about by a familiar, once known passion Jack quickly hung up the phone, playfully manipulating Laurie into accepting his request.

"Jack, no! Jack!" *Dammit*, she thought to herself, realizing he was off the phone already as she brought her fist forcefully upon the desktop. *Damn him*, she thought. She sat at her desk, sighed and shook her head.

– – –

The next day Laurie had become much more at ease about her upcoming meeting with Jack. She knew all too well that there existed a part of herself that was drowned in curiosity and laden with temptation that desperately wished to see Jack again. So she gave in, secretly and with extreme caution, she gave in.

Jack of course had serendipitously, haphazardly fallen back into Laurie's life and he knew that in such an instance as this fate shone just to strong to be reflected and ignored. So he smiled as his plane landed in Seattle and turned on his cellular phone to a smorgasbord of angry text messages and voice mails from his beloved brother, Stan. Most of them were to the tune of, WHY THE HELL DID YOU BLOW OFF THE DENVER STOP ON THE TOUR AND WHERE IN GOD'S NAME ARE YOU?? CALL ME NOW JACK!!!!

Jack laughed quietly to himself before standing up to de-board the plane. It was the type of laugh congruent with a shrug of the shoulders, a simple chuckle that Jack had become quite familiar with using in conversations with his brother. Perhaps it was never the best idea to employ his younger brother. Jack had been told this many times, by many people, but as with most things Jack chose to put their opinions on mute and go about his affairs strictly as he pleased. Even on the days that Jack regretted having his little brother manage his career, he was shortly thereafter rest assured with the fact that he had helped his younger brother experience the better things in life. Jack had done just that, too. He had in the truth of the matter supplied his brother with a career that made money a distant struggle of the past and allowed him to spend the most of his time as he pleased, that is, when he was not busy battling with Jack over deadlines and skipped appearances.

Jack and Stan had a common male sibling relationship. They fought, they argued, swore to themselves they were done with one the other and then forgotten it all and vowed eternally to always take care of each other, no matter what the circumstances. Just like the brotherly bonds between other brothers here, there and throughout time and space these two were not unique in the fact that they would always share a connection and a love that could never be broken. Thus, they constantly looked out for the other and kept each other's best interests steadfast in mind. Or, at least what each believed to be such.

Even though Stan was angry with Jack for completely missing his scheduled appearance in Denver, Jack knew all too well that he would get over his current grievance and once again be back on his side. Surely enough, Jack would be correct. Stan would never stay mad at him for long simply because Jack had always made sure his brother was always taken care of.

To Jack, it was not just about financially helping his younger sibling. To him, it was about much more. He wanted more than anything, for Stan, as he did with all the people he came across in life, to realize and understand that life needed to be enjoyed and celebrated. He never wanted his brother to have to work thanklessly for some arrogant bastard who had become so consumed with his own problems and stresses that he had come to be washed up and wrung out in misery and hatefulness. More than anything though, Jack protested strongly against Stan becoming that bastard.

Just as he had looked out for Stan and others close to him in this way, he now more than ever felt the need to help Laurie understand that her life was in dire need of reassessment. He remembered Laurie, clearly and unfiltered from years ago. He knew the moment he saw her, the moment she spoke and looked at him with fossilized, stony eyes that the real Laurie Dreusel was fading away and taking with her her own happiness and value of life. Jack did not plan on harping down on Laurie, telling her she was a fraud, that she was living for the wrong reasons. Although that was exactly what she expected of Jack, that was the one thing he refused to do. Instead, he would attempt to win her over by showing her the good in life and inspiring her to find that good. That was Jack's forte. It was how he got so many fans and avid followers of his philosophy to take up a lifestyle that catered to each man's most personal and intimate desires. Just as Jack had a confidence evident in almost all things he did, he was sure that he could persuade Laurie to get back in touch with a seemingly forgotten side of herself.

As Jack thought about this he trailed deeper into thought, gliding through the airport terminals he thought more and more about the Laurie Dreusel he had known and loved. He could remember her long, dark hair that had seemed to lighten, shorten and dry out considerably since he last saw her. He remembered her, sitting on their worn out polyester couch that they shared in their small one bedroom apartment, smoking her cigarette, holding her beer and laughing infectiously after every other sentence spoken. He could see her in crystal vision, picking her guitar back up after the cigarette was out and composing a sweet and simple melody accompanied by improvised, silly and humorous lyrics that had every person sitting in the room won over with a gentle laughter. The feeling those memories gave Jack had all the sensation of a gulp of whiskey that warms the entire body with a toasty array of flavor and delight. Those memories warmed him inside, a heat he could feel through his entire body, starting at the pit of his stomach and extending outward to his limbs, securing his whole existence with feelings of pleasure and pure delight. With that thought, with that reminiscent feeling of spicy bourbon running through his bloodstream, Jack stopped at an airport bar to meet up with his fair-weather friend before exiting the terminal. There he struck up a conversation with the lonely bartender, telling him about his reasons for gracing Seattle with his presence and sharing with him the saga of Laurie and himself.

# CHAPTER FIVE

Laurie was preparing for her dinner with Jack. She had gone out earlier that day to purchase a short and slimming, low-cut, black dress that loudly whispered *take me*. She had curled her hair and put it up, nice and high, with only a few solemn strands sliding down the curves of her cheekbones. Looking in the mirror she grinned, it was a smile that exposed an inner existence which she had kept hidden for so long. It screamed in glory, in ecstasy, passion, love and desire. It screamed and squealed, bellowed and profoundly proclaimed her true feelings kept inside. This time, she was not frightened by the omniscient smile on her face. As she gazed into her reflection she permitted herself a glimpse at her true self. Again she smiled, at first at the image she saw in the mirror and then again as she saw the inner side of herself forcing itself out as her smile grew wider and fuller across her tanned face. Although she knew she was grotesquely glamorous on the outside, what delighted her the most was what she saw in that smile. She was finally witness to her own emotions. Those emotions humbled her. Though she had spent so many years by Jack's side, though they had experienced and learned so much together, despite the fact that each knew the others inner workings like father time knows the burrows of a clock, Laurie was still nervous to be in his presence.

So she fixed herself up more so than she ever would for a typical night on the town, on the prowl for a fool like Tom who set out as a predator and ended up defenseless prey. It was those Toms that Laurie would dress up for, she had to. To them it was a game of rouse and mystique, the most seductive girl in the bar, the biggest lips, the largest breasts, the most beautiful Betty. Laurie knew if she wanted to reel in one of those men she would have to look her best. Yet even for them she never took the time she did this evening. In years she had not so meticulously placed every strand of curled hair in its specific place nor had she spent four hours in one store searching for the perfect dress to be worn that same evening. Jack had never worried about materialistic nonsense such as that. Laurie knew that, too. She knew all her hours spent on sprucing up for him were effortless, they always had been. Jack had never cared how Laurie's hair looked, how low-cut her dress was or how good her ass looked in the ensemble she was wearing. If Laurie had been wearing a greasy wife-beater and a baggy pair of oversized sweat pants, not showered in a week and had hair that strayed in all directions he would have been just as turned on. Still, she perfected her look until it seemed flawless. Oddly enough she wanted to be her very best for the one man she knew would take her whole-heartedly at her very worst.

She waited for Jack at the posh restaurant which she had set up reservations with. It was a quarter after and they had scheduled to meet at eight. Laurie pushed the fears lingering in her head that Jack would be a no-show away. She closed her eyes and took a glass of merlot from the smiling waiter as she nervously checked the time on her cell phone again. 8:16, it read. She sipped the wine as her face formed a bitter pucker after realizing the sip had turned into somewhat of a chug. Her so called anxiety began to surface as she imagined Jack strolling the streets with the redhead she had seen him backstage with. *He wouldn't blow me off,* she thought. *He couldn't.* As nervous as she was about the dinner with Jack, she remained overly confident in her seductive prowess. She raised her chin slightly higher, arrogantly smiled, looked in the mirror hanging on a wall adjacent to her and held up her wine glass as she snottily beckoned the waiter for a refill.

When she saw Jack enter the main door at the front of the restaurant she quickly reached in her handbag for the prescription bottle she never let out of her close grasp. Her hands were shaking as she unscrewed the bottle underneath the table and grabbed two Xanex from the container. She swallowed them both without hesitation and glanced up at Jack as the hostess showed him to Laurie's table. The second pill had become lodged in her throat as Jack began to take his seat and she pounded her chest to loosen the medication from her esophagus. Quickly he stood up.

"You alright?" He asked, a bit startled.

Clearing her throat and taking a sip of water she answered, "Sure. Strong wine, that's all."

He studied her face as he sat down. He allowed his amicable smile to hide the distress he felt inside. It was her face. The slender chin, high cheekbones, supple and plump lips. It was recognizable at first glance. Not even the footprints of age could make her unfamiliar in even the strongest sense. Though tanned considerably more than he had ever imagined or would have fathomed, her face remained the same. The lines and curves were still angular and sharp yet yielded a softness that called in the looker's eyes as sirens beckoning from rocky shores.

Her eyes were what he immediately focused on. He could not at first put his finger on what was so different about them. They were still blue and glowing with a dark border around the effervescently colored iris. Their intensity was magnified only more by the snowy white backdrop that hung behind them. As he stared at them with an actor's smile, he was puzzled as to what had changed.

"So, how was your flight?" She opened the conversation with a bubbly, upbeat tone.

"The flight. Yeah, it was fine." He searched for words to say as he curiously looked at Laurie. His facetious smile tuned into a flirtatious smirk. Still, he remained muddled and at a loss.

They chatted with each other as the appetizers came and went. They talked mostly about Jack's life as an author and about his many travels, since that was after all the purpose of the meeting. As much as he tried to turn the subject towards Laurie, she resisted and quickly turned the conversation back on him. It was then when he started to understand that the barrier he had come across would be harder to tear down than he thought. This was surely not the same Laurie. The realization saddened him. As he tried to act as though nothing was bothering him in even the slightest, as he tried desperately to redraw the smile on his face every second, his disappointment finally took the reigns and troubled eyes appeared upon his once charismatic face.

Not even taking notice in his demeanor, Laurie continued eating her scallops and shrimp while droning on with boring, meaningless questions such as, "So what do you do when you aren't working, Jack?"

The lines sounded rehearsed and Jack was put off completely. Finally, he interrupted Laurie in the midst of her next question and brazenly asked, "What is keeping you so unhappy?"

Stunned, she looked back with a doped up glaze painted on her face. "What?" she asked defensively.

"Sorry doll, but you aren't happy. It took me a minute to notice but..."

"Not happy? My life is freaking perfect Jack."

"Sure, if you say so. But I just don't see it. I don't see happiness in you anymore."

"Well, maybe to you life is all about galavanting around the world, careless and fancy free. Well for the rest of us we actually have to work. And yes, I am happy. Very happy for your information. I just got a raise, a promotion, I live in a great condo, make a great living and have everything I could ever need. So how dare you tell me I'm not happy."

"Ok, take it easy, I'm not trying to offend you."

"Offend me? Please. How would I possibly be offended by some sleazy Stanford dropout who's lain on his ass half his life and for some fucked off reason came across a streak of luck that got him some fancy book deal and plopped a fortune right in his lap. No, Jack, I actually worked for my money. You are just another lazy jerk who thinks everything will just magically come to you because you are so clever and so smart. Well it's luck Jack, that's all it is. Luck comes and goes. What I have is not luck. It's dedication, it's skill, it's discipline. Just because you could never learn any of those concepts and somehow made it on your own does not now, and will never, put you on a pedestal!"

With that she threw her napkin on the table, pushed back her chair and stood up. Jack had a minuscule, slightly cockeyed grin on his face.

"Yeah, smile. That's your defense for everything isn't it? I can't wait to write this feature on you that's for sure. It'll be out next week, look for it! Or actually, don't. It will probably just boost your ego further in some strange way."

As she walked away from the table and into the main lobby towards the doors, Jack hung his head to hide a subtle laughter and an unyielding smile. He had figured it out, Laurie was hopelessly miserable yet could not admit it to even herself.

# CHAPTER SIX

    After the drama filled attempt at dinner, Jack waited a few hours before calling Laurie. There was no answer. She had already made it home and was now on her way to her favorite uptown bar. He walked around the Seattle streets, scuffing his shoes against the concrete, one hand in his pocket and the other brushing through his hair frequently. Although he was now sure of what seemed so different about Laurie that evening he was still confused as to how she became that way.

He could remember her back in college years. She was loving, fun, simple and above all happy. He began to think that perhaps he had seen it coming. He felt as though maybe he should have done something about it near the end of their time together when she was constantly stressing over what he considered unimportant and obsolete. But, he let her go the day she decided to end it all. He had seen it coming for months and did nothing to stop it. Jack loved Laurie devoutly and knew he would be broken to some degree by their parting. It was a pain he had felt before and was sure he would feel again. So even though the thought of her absent from his life was at the time mildly nauseating and warranted many restless nights, Jack refused to change his ideals or lifestyle in order to live by anyone else's terms. So when she gave him the ultimatum and threatened to leave, he swallowed the lump in his throat and let her go.

He blamed the ways of the world. *Poor, naïve Laurie,* he thought. He felt as though she had been made victim to the facetiousness and hatred in the world around her. He knew she wanted to be accepted, liked and looked up to. Laurie had always wanted people to like her. That was never an obstacle for her either. Intensity shone through her vivid eyes and people were spellbound in her presence. Or, at least once that was the case. Times had changed drastically since those days, though. Jack knew that her ambitious drive to be accepted was indeed part responsible for molding the woman Laurie had now become. He knew that drive had blindly forced her to take bidding in all the nonsense thrown at her by magazines, TV shows, commercials and every other media outlet that existed. She had to feel as though she was doing it right and everyone around her was proud. If she could be like the 21st century poster-children she saw with every corner she turned and every magazine page she flipped through then she had made it  and everything had worked out perfectly.

Jack wondered something else as he scooted his feet slowly down the sidewalk. He wondered why it bothered him so much that she had become this way. He could see bitterness in her that never before existed. It was bitterness fueled by misery. He knew she was unaware that she was unhappy too, but he could not understand why he cared so much. Jack was used to coming across those who had been worn down and reprogrammed by society's expectations. Though those were the ones he preached to in his novels and on stage, it really never mattered to him whether they changed or not. He was happy and he felt that simply telling people how to be as carefree as him was simply enough. Never did those people who spent hundreds on his books and seminars only to turn right back to their prison like lives have any affect on him. Laurie did. What bothered him the most about it was that he felt helpless. He was truly unsure of whether or not he could help her change back into the girl he knew she so desperately needed to be.

With that thought Jack stopped and sat on the curb of the street corner. A suave looking gentleman in a suit walked out of the bar he was stooped next to and waited as the valet brought his car. Looking back at the bar and then once again at the gently lit street, he stood up and approached the front glass windows of the establishment. *Paulie's*, the paint on the door read in white, cursive letters. Surely, he thought, there would be no cheap drink specials at this joint. Inside women were dressed in sleek, classy get-ups with designer heels and small sparkly clutches. Men wore mostly suits. Jack laughed, almost silently under his breath, before deciding to amuse himself and walk inside.

Inside the bar he took a seat next to a man, who like him, seemed to be out of his element in the current surroundings. He wore jeans and a long sleeved t-shirt. As his shirt sleeve slid up his arm Jack could see the brightly colored labyrinth of tattooed artwork covering his skin. He nodded to the man and offered a casual greeting. With that the stranger held out his hand towards Jack and introduced himself as Spence.

"Short for Spencer," he added, "what do you drink?"

"Whiskey on the rocks. Always." Jack replied.

"Good. It's on me. Hey, babe," he said, summoning the bartender over before he ordered Jack's drink.

The dark haired woman behind the bar smiled sweetly at Jack and slid the drink to him.

"Thanks sweetheart," the man named Spence said to her before blowing a subtle wink her way.

"So you're here often I take it?" Jack asked.

"Well yeah, that's my wife so I guess that makes me a regular."

"Okay, I was going to say you didn't seem to be the average Joe in this place. No offense or anything like that."

"Tell me about it," he said chuckling as he glanced around the dimly lit room.

The two men talked while sipping their liquor. They conversed about simple matters as they warmed up to one another. Soon enough the topic turned to Jack's line of work.

"Oh yeah, I've heard about you. Somewhere, maybe the radio or a billboard. Anyway good for you, man," Spence said, raising his glass to Jack.

As Jack clung glasses with his newfound acquaintance he brought up Laurie and his grievance with her that began earlier that day.

"Well what makes you so sure she's really not happy? I mean just because she doesn't follow your philosophy on what happiness means?"

"Well no, I mean, I don't know, I can just, well, I can see it in her eyes, you know." He choked on his words slightly.

"Right. But do you really think that means that she's unhappy because of her career and the way she lives her life, like you were saying?"

"Well, I think so. She was happy once, when I knew her forever ago."

"And people change. With that, their perception of happiness changes too."

Jack paused for a moment, tilted his head like a labrador questioning his master's commands and licked his lips all while looking Spence right in the eyes and responded, "I, I guess you'd be right."

"Well I'm just saying what makes you happy may not be right for the next guy."

"Yeah, but who wouldn't want to make a living doing just what they want, no real schedule. Just come and go as you please?" Jack debated.

"Sure, sounds good. But what about all the workaholics? I mean the guys who don't do it for the money. Their schedule makes them happy. They love working, that's their thing." Spence rebutted in a calm, matter of fact tone. His argument set no thick air as that of a heated discussion. He was confident and convincing. His sturdy voice produced a wisdom that Jack had rarely come across.

Jack turned back around on his barstool to face the shelves of liquor, layered and lit up from the bottom of the platforms they sat upon. He sipped his whiskey twice before softly answering, "Touche my friend, touche."

# CHAPTER SEVEN

Much later that night Laurie sat at the bar in the quaint, uptown venue she favored sipping a dry martini and dabbing her lip with a printed napkin that read *Paulie's*. It was her second since she had arrived but thirty minutes ago and she surely showed no signs that it would be her last. She chatted flirtatiously with the gentleman sitting to her left. He was about thirty-five, tall with dark hair and an agitated woman by his side. The woman constantly touched his leg for attention, yet he ignored her subtle nudges and focused all his attention on Laurie. Noticing this, Laurie smiled with pride as she looked around the room quickly only to purposefully meet eyes with the blonde two seats away and give her a boastful, egotistical smirk.

Suddenly she looked to the entrance as she heard a familiar voice. Her eyes followed him as he walked in the doors and around the bar, at once realizing that the familiar voice was accompanied by an all too familiar face. It was Tom. This did not surprise Laurie since she was used to seeing her so called buddy about this time of night and at this place. She looked at him seductively as he took a seat with the brunette woman whom he walked into the bar with. He caught her attention-demanding glance and excused himself from his date to make his way to Laurie.

"Come have a drink with us, doll."

The word doll resonated with Laurie as it hauntingly called Jack back into her conscience. She stood up with out so much as an excuse to the man next to her and joined Tom and his female friend at the opposite side of the bar. Just like she had with the agitated woman still sitting across from her,

Laurie gave a venomous smirk to the brunette on Tom's left side. It was the type of smirk that exhumed confidence and cockiness and was intended to make any catching it feel slightly less than. When Tom and other men just like him would take the bait, Laurie would swoop in for the steal if for no other reason than to make herself feel wanted and desired.

She had the need to feel wanted since leaving Jack. Maybe it was his laissez-faire attitude about the topic of dating or maybe it was the various meaningless flings he would have right in front of Laurie's eyes, but either way she was always secretly vying for his undivided attention. He couldn't understand what bothered her so much about this all. The other women seemed irrelevant to him as he thought she knew that love and sex were completely separate entities in his mind. Maybe if only to attract him in the first place Laurie had led Jack to believe these were her philosophies too, and with that a match was made. As time went on it only bothered Laurie more that she couldn't be his only even if in his mind she was. So she left him in search of a more mature and committed relationship which she never seemed to find. As the realization settled that it was simply a rat race she had become consumed by in search of a viable mate she ironically enough started to adhere to Jack's philosophy on intimacy at last.

Around three in the morning Laurie slunk out of Tom's bed, gently and discreetly, being sure to not wake him or the brunette from the bar who lay there asleep as well.

Without much shut-eye Laurie set out early the next day to get to the office and start hacking away at Jack's follow up article. Perhaps it was once again the craving to be wanted oh so badly or maybe it was just the bad taste of a stale threesome left in Laurie's mouth, but either way something bothered her intensely this morning. Although angered by every bit of the situation she would never let on to any of this. No, she would just take it out on her keyboard, the only witness to all that underlying self pity and hatred other than herself. Even better? She had to write about Jack. Jack, the one who had fueled it all. Had he taken part in molding any of the woman she had become today? She refused to believe it. She refused to believe that any similarities they shared regarding love, sex or intimacy were at all existent. She was going to prove it to the world, too. Well, at least to the greater Seattle area that is.

After nearly four cups of coffee, drank only to hide the fact that she was on a self-medicated regimen of barbiturates, and a quite hazy two and a half hours later Laurie leaned back in her swiveling desk chair, clicked SEND, sighed and grinned. With a real mean-girl sort of attitude and a conspicuous cockiness in her demeanor Laurie strutted her way through the hallways and straight out the door of the tall building that housed Seattle's number one selling newspaper.

Sitting under the familiar, dimmed bar lights and starting on her second martini, dry and strong, Laurie began to feel the creeping sensation of regret seep into her pores. She gulped the martini, squinted her eyes as she did it and tilted her head back as she took another hardy swig.

"Screw him, he deserves it," she told herself, gaining the bartender's attention.

"What, doll?"

With that word Laurie grunted, finished her martini at mach speed and laid a twenty on the bar as she gave a look to her fair-weather server friend that sort of said goodbye.

Refusing to let herself feel at all guilty for the unflattering article she had just spat out about Jack, Laurie lay down on her 1200 thread-count egyptian cotton couch with a package of rice cakes, a homemade vodka tonic and the oversized TV turned to her favorite mindless reality show. With that she was thereby shortly tuned out of her real world problems and once again had drifted off to her materialistic, superficial la-la land. Once the program had ended and the vodka was sipped dry Laurie picked up the phone to call Jack. She dialed the number and immediately got his voicemail. Unhinged she left a quick, cheerful message about how his newest feature article would be out tomorrow and she would be more than happy to send him a copy.

# CHAPTER EIGHT

Laurie waited the next morning, anxiously anticipating her cellphone's annoying little melody to disturb the uninterrupted silence. But nothing. She could not figure out why he hadn't called her furious, angry, demanding an explanation or apology for her damaging little expose. But no, nothing. Even by noon the phone had not rang once nor had an email from Jack come through. For Laurie would know if it had, she had checked every fifteen to twenty minutes, tapping her phone's screen to see if she had somehow missed a call. She had not.

*Well he obviously hasn't read it,* she comforted herself. *He would have called complaining if he had. Right?* Before long Laurie found herself whittling away the day obsessing over Jack's reaction to the piece.

Unfolding the weekend paper she flipped through it, section by section, until she found her self-proclaimed masterpiece. She read the words in an almost completely muted voice over and over again. It began:

*Meet Jack Foster, a man that many have put much of their faith in. So much faith that some have quit their jobs, spent their hard-earned income and eventually lost everything because of an unrealistic dream that Foster has made millions believe. Yet this pipe dream will never come true. His banter and charm have fooled many and swooped each into a whirlwind of promises of wealth, success and happiness, only for them to be let down in the end with the costs greatly outweighing the benefits. Foster is nothing short of a con-artist as he willingly makes millions each year believe that he has the secret to success, when really his story is a fraud.*

The article went on to expose every black speck scattered across Jack's past. From his days of recreational drug use and carefree behavior in college before dropping out of Stanford to his modern day womanizing ways. That was not the harshest of it all, either. Laurie really let it all run out on this one. All the emotions, all the years of anger, of denial, of hatred and self loathing. All of it came out, word by ruthless word, tearing into Jack in greasy black ink for any to see and read that Saturday morning.

Finally she gave in and picked up the phone to call Jack. No answer. By the next day when she still had not heard from him, she picked up the phone with jagged nails that had recently been chewed to the tips and dialed his number.

"Hey-lo."

"Hi, Jack, it's Laurie." And with out so much as a half second's delay she went right into the reason she was calling, "I was just seeing if you had gotten a copy of your feature? It went out yesterday." A malicious and manipulative grin presented itself behind puckered lips as the words came out.

"Yeah, yeah. I read that."

"And?" she demanded

"Yeah, uh not too shabby, doll. It's about time someone stopped kissing my ass in these damn reviews. I mean, the people gotta know the truth right?"

"So. You're okay with it? You didn't find it, oh I don't know, too harsh or damaging?"

"Damaging? Oh that's a good one. No, doll, I pay no mind to these little things you know this. Plus, I'm sure you had to put that spin on it to sell a few more papers," his tone was neither aggravated nor did it display the slightest hint of animosity. Instead, he responded softly and in his trademark jovial, laissez-faire voice.

Laurie was pissed. "Right. Well good. Good then. Just making sure. Gotta run though." *Click.*

"Ok, dol..." He looked at the phone with a smile sheltering defeat. *How had she become so calloused?* This thought plagued him for hours after that call. He could hear it in her voice, her anger, her denial, the self-loathing and hatred she had given into in hopes of making her self what others so desperately wanted her to be. *Had I hurt her that badly so long ago? Is that why she's like this now? Am I missing something?* He wondered. He wondered and wondered as he analyzed thought after repeating thought that was infused with a stinging pain that was only softened with the malty elixir that sat shelved in the top cabinet in his kitchen.

Back in Seattle Laurie was still fuming. Her phone, now broken after being flung across the room lay next to a shattered drinking glass and spilled orange juice. The fact that Jack had simply shrugged off her devastating little expose tore into her more violently than top force winds during a category five twister. She sat down and cried. For the first time in a while, Laurie felt tears flow helplessly out of her, drenching her further in her own self disdain. Reminding her with every drop that she had lost the battle, that Jack had won. Him, the one who did it all wrong, who never played by the rules while she had given up everything to do just that. He had what she wanted. It wasn't money, it wasn't fame or even prestige for that matter. It was the simple feeling of contentment. The most basic of human emotions. The most essential component to life. The one thing Laurie was almost completely void of. The tears served as a haunting reminder of the life she had given up so long ago. Not a life with Jack, but a life with happiness. Each tear forced her to admit more and more shamefully to herself that she was indeed miserable. Maybe it was the fact that she had not allowed herself to cry or even show much emotion over the last few years, but each drip, drip, drop down the side of her slender cheek bones dissolved her into the reality of what her life had become.

She still did not understand how he could laugh it off so easily. *Did he not care what people thought? Even if their opinion was that of a fraud and a liar?* She guessed not, but that just angered her more. So as she sat stagnant on the floor, drowning in her own misery, she began to wonder if anyone else would really care either. Again, she guessed the answer was no.

# CHAPTER NINE

The next morning Laurie was called into her editor's office. Waiting patiently for him to arrive, she looked around the familiar office that was swarming with mahogany furniture and needless photos of his oh so dear family. She smiled a little as she remembered Stephanie and her cool, relaxing charm that graced the office and ultimately the chase lounge adjacent to Dave Novell's desk. Laurie knew

Dave well and knew the error of his ways. Even though she despised him for what he was she kissed his righteous ass sweetly and thoroughly because, well, that's what your supposed to do if you want to make it in this world. Or so she had been trained.

As she sat in the black leather seat surrounded by brass studs that clung onto the wood frame for dear life she chewed her nails some more, hoping to fix the previously done damage. Dave walked in the door.

"Ah, Laurie, Laurie." He grabbed her face and kissed her on the nose as she puckered her lips back in fear of tasting his stale, coffee soaked breath.

She looked at him smiling, yet puzzled.

"Well! Good job, kid! Get up and congratulate yourself. Didn't think ya had it in ya."

"Right, well I was hoping you wouldn't find the piece too, well, um, harsh? I know you like the guy."

"Harsh? You're kidding me right? You know how many papers we've sold? You know how many people in the Seattle area are gonna swoop this up and revolt after they read what this asshole did to them?" Dave circled around the room, coffee cup in hand as he bellowed his praised to Laurie.

"Well good then, glad you're happy, Dave." She smiled a smile that couldn't have look more fake on the next Miss America. "I, I thought you liked him though? Isn't that why you had me cover him in the first place?"

"Like him! Ha! I've never despised a man so much in all my life. You know what he's done to these people? Terrible, terrible. You have to write more about it."

"Write more, but Dave, it's just that, well, there's nothing more to say."

"Nothing more? There's plenty more! We will pollute the airwaves with this! It will be the next big scandal! Tell ya what, we are even going to set up a seminar. Yes, a seminar, right here in Seattle for Mr. Foster to speak at where all the scammed fans of his can come and demand their money back! Think of the press now!"

Although Dave's face was positioned towards the outward facing window, Laurie could see the gleam in his eye. It took her a minute to respond. She was almost dumbfounded.

"So, you want me to find some more negative press on him then?"

"What don't you get, kid! Find everything you can, include it your next big feature. I'll start working on this seminar shit right away and let you know the dates. Knew you were right for this kid, knew ya had it in ya."

He came over to Laurie and hugged her before slapping her on the ass, something he had never done. Surprised, she scooted out the door wondering what the hell just happened.

# CHAPTER TEN

By next Friday the seminar had been set up. Jack was due to arrive in Seattle once again the following week. Laurie was lost in a bout of confusion. She couldn't fathom what had come to be. Now there she was, helpless as she faced a decision between advancing her career or advancing her true self. It was a decision that was never so difficult for her to make. For once, moral complexity overshadowed her ambition and greed. This only disoriented her more.

Jack, unaware of the trap he was set to walk into, was anxious for his upcoming meeting with Laurie. Confusion plagued him too, however his was based solely on the fact that he could not quite put his finger on why Laurie's apparent sadness bothered him in such a way. He had to see her. Not for love, not for rekindling of ant sort but simply to convince himself that he was not the one who bruised her so badly. He refused to believe that she had just become such a wretched person on her own accord.

Before long the days had dwindled down to the following Friday. Jack's plane would be landing in a matter of mere hours. Laurie tapped her fingers nervously on her desk as she looked at the clock. Second by agonizing second ticked by until Laurie's anticipation gave in. She swiftly picked up her desk phone and hit her editor's extension to inform him she was done and would be leaving for the day.

"Uh, sure kid, why don't you come in here for a sec first."

"Of course, right away, Dave," her short professional tone rattled through the receiving end.

Walking halfway through the door, Laurie stopped and peeked her head in the mahogany drenched office.

"Come in, come in," Dave said as he leaned back in his plush leather chair and loosened his already distraught looking tie.

There was an unfamiliar vibe in the air that Laurie could undeniably sense. It was a vibe she had never before gotten from Dave. No, not from Dave but from nameless other men in authoritative positions just like him. Men she had once tangled with in white cotton sheets in effort to grab hold to any ounce of power and success dripping out of them. It took her a few seconds but she soon recognized that pompous ass smirk and those inglorious gleaming eyes that shimmered in the same way as when an old, lonely man just Dave Novell had come across the mecca of free internet porn. Laurie came in, shut the door behind her and without so much as thinking about her next move slightly undid the top button to her blouse. Walking towards him she ran her fingers through her flowing hair and sat down on the other side of Dave's desk. Before she could take notice of her actions she was already sliding her knee-length skirt up her tanned, smooth leg. It had become all to much of a habit, the look, the smirk. It all triggered her instantly to act as she had with so many other men. To her, it was just another tactical skill needed to climb a very high ladder in her life.

"So, kid, are you ready for tomorrow? I know you've got this in the bag. You've always had that, well, something special about you. Know what I mean?"

"No, Dave, what *do* you mean?" She spoke softly and subtly in an intoxicating tone as she leaned over to show a ray of cleavage.

Dave got up from his desk, walked around to Laurie's side and put his hand on her shoulder. It was all too cliche. However, this never really mattered to Laurie. No, the romance novel affairs and unrealistic Merlot soaked fantasies never bored her. Perhaps it was because that carnal attraction, that undeniable lust present in nearly every heart and soul was the only true emotion of hers that was tangible in her self-pity marinated world. So she let her poisoned mind speak over her troubled self and leaned towards Dave with her take me now smile.

Then, the phone rang. The loud, echoing nuisance immediately shook away the Danielle Steele like passion which was now lying thick in the air. Dave patted her shoulder endearingly before going to answer the phone and shooing Laurie away with his hand  before he was quickly back to business.

She buttoned her shirt before leaving the office with so much as a glance back at her editor.

Once at home Laurie poured herself her usual. She paced around her apartment as she rehearsed a somewhat sincere sounding apology to Jack. She wondered if she should even apologize for her last piece, after all had he really taken it to heart? It didn't seem to bother him, or so he had made it seem over the phone. Laurie refused to believe it. Her liquored up ego and boosted confidence as a result of the flirtation with Dave earlier that day soon convinced her that she had obviously hurt him. She smiled her maniacal smile as she flung her martini glass around the room just before picking up her newest over priced cellular phone and scrolling down the contact list to press the send button once the cursor landed over the name *Tom Moore.*

# CHAPTER ELEVEN

The next morning's sun glared into Laurie's window through the crack in her curtain. It woke her only a few hours after she had lain down in her bed, drunk, alone and full of herself. She quickly rolled out of bed and began her day with little attention to her subtle, seemingly routine hangover. It then dawned on her that morning she would see Jack.

At the convention hall Laurie waited in the lobby. She had taken her Xanex so any unwanted nervousness slowly melted away with her headache as she coached herself on exactly how to act in front of Jack. On the outside Laurie looked patient and calm but her subconscious knew it was but an act, just like the one she was soon to put on. Her insecurity and self hatred plagued her deeply, but the frothy haze of the heavy barbiturates set in and now she was just as good as fucking golden.

Jack walked in through the double doors directly adjacent from where Laurie was seated. She stared for what to her seemed like minutes as she noticed the cool, collected charm that radiated out of him. His suit was not too domineering, his hair was a bit scruffy and a very slight but still conspicuous five O'Clock shadow highlighted his jowl. It was Jack alright. Laurie was once again diseased with jealousy as she looked straight at him, standing there with his hang loose attitude and school-boy smile.

He soon noticed her sitting and as he walked over to her slowly she rushed up with a hand placed outward.

"Jack."

"Laurie," he said looking at her hand with a raised eyebrow before placing it between both of his and patting it on top.

"Well!" She smiled. "Are you ready for today?"

"Yeah, sure, ready as I'll ever be."

He noticed Laurie had done away with her self righteous attitude and condescending mannerisms. Although she adorned a bright, white toothed smile and apparent newfound happiness Jack felt something was just not right. He looked into her mildly glassy eyes as he tried to keep a friendly smile on his face.

Silence stood thick for a moment. It was not an awkward silence but simply one with a disheartened heaviness, such as that evident at the funeral of a loved one. They both took notice.

As the two of them walked backstage neither Laurie nor Jack were at all aware of the chaos that was soon to ensue. Though Dave had pranced around the office, bellowing praises and seeing dollar signs, Laurie was too caught up in her own self-involved world that she failed to realize his ramblings just may have been something she should have taken to heart.

"You, know, Jack, the article, it, well it was all about business."

"Got ya, doll," he said with a dispirited leer.

"Right, well, like I said before, no hard feelings?"

"Nope. None here."

"Good, good then." She nodded and smiled politely.

The conversation seemed almost alien to them both. Short, to the point and business like. It was not that neither of them noticed it, nor was it something both of them at the time could put their finger on. Jack however, had a faint hint that it was the fact that both of them were displeased with what Laurie had grown into since days spent at Stanford University.

Again, the silence stood thick until Jack's brother walked into the room.

"Ok, you've got an hour," he ordered Jack.

"Stan, Stan my man, you remember Laurie Dreusel, right?"

"Bock, it's Bock now," she broke in as she stood to greet Stan.

Stan froze for a moment as he looked at Jack with widened eyes.

"Relax, Stan, don't get too excited, she's only covering the seminar today," he spoke affably and with a slight laughter in his speech.

"Right, Laurie. Laurie Bock. Well, good to see you again, dear. Read that last story you did on Jack here," Stan said in an accusing tone.

"Just my job, you know. No hard feelings though." She stretched her hand out to meet Stan's. He ignored her polite gesture.

"Jack, can I talk to you a second, privately?" He glared at Laurie.

"Nonsen..." Jack began to blurt out before Laurie excused herself and left the back room.

"What the hell, Jack? You can't let her cover you again. You know how many angry calls I've gotten from folks around here since her last write up on you?" Stan circled the room, hand on balding head, as he lectured Jack.

"Stan, Stan, it's fine. No publicity is the only bad publicity, isn't that what you say?"

"Yeah, well, bad publ..."

Jack cut in, "angry fans, huh? Well what on Earth are they angry about?" Jack's question was sincere.

"Jack! They think you've scammed them! That you're a fraud! Jesus! I was hoping this seminar would help boost your image with this demographic again. But now that *she's* covering it, good fucking luck!"

"Relax, relax. It will be fine. She even apologized for the last one, it was just what her editor asked of her, that's all."

"I don't know, Jack, I don't know. This could be bad. Real fucking bad!"

Jack couldn't understand why Stan was so worried. "Well why didn't you say something before now?"

"Oh, I didn't want to worry you, stress you out, I don't know! That was before I knew *she'd* be here!"

"Would you stop saying she like that? It will be okay, Stan, trust me." He grabbed his little brother by the shoulders in a comforting response but Stan was not reassured.

"Do you even remember what she did to you, Jack, years ago?"

Jack's amiable laugh broke through the tension. "Stan, that was so long ago. You really need to relax. I'm fine. It will be fine. And who cares anyway, it's just Seattle."

Stan shook his head, still unconvinced but with no way of possibly getting through to his stubborn older brother.

– – –

The door to the back room opened and Jack found Laurie standing in the hallway, prescription bottle in hand. Instantly the glazed over look in her face and her untroubled stance made sense to Jack. He welcomed her back into the room as Stan left with a dagger like look he projected in

Laurie's direction. The time leading up to Jack's appearance on stage was spent over a very formal conversation between the two. He almost couldn't stand it anymore. He would have much rather had Laurie's true self come out, even if it rendered emotions of anger, detestation and hostility. He wanted to see them, in every true form of themselves, only to further analyze her misery correctly. Before long the boring conversation had melted down the minutes and Jack was due in front of his audience in five.

As he left the room and walked down the hallway with Stan, his little brother noticed a deflated energy in Jack's step.

"Everything okay? You alright? What happened in there?" Stan asked impatiently.

"What, oh, nothing. Nope, all good." He smiled.

Moments later Jack walked towards his podium by entering through the left wing of the stage. At once a few stood up and before his first sentence could begin a man yelled, "I want my money back!"

Jack iced up if for but only a second before beginning his seminar.

"Well, hello there. How's it going Seattle? I can see we have some questions, we'll get to those later, buddy." He pointed and winked at the dissatisfied attendee.

"Fuck you!" The man yelled before a security officer stationed at the back came to escort him out of the convention hall.

Jack gulped as he looked at the stoic faces staring upwards at him. He went on.

"Well, like many of you sitting out there today, I once wondered what *success* would *really* feel like. I didn't want to give my life away for it either. I needed an answer."

A woman stood up from the front row and without hesitation screamed out, "Liar!" Another at her side immediately stood by her, hand raised in the air and wailed "Fake! You're a fake!"

Jack had stopped talking by now.

"What did the over 1500 bucks I've spent on your damn books and seminars do for me?" The first lady bellowed again.

"I see we have some doubters in the crowd. That's ok, success comes in strides, this is what is important to remember. You see, you can't expect it all at once."

"I've spent hundreds on your worthless books and bullshit!" This time the outburst came from a stalky, bald man who reminded Jack somewhat of his brother. This man, however, was in much worse shape. A disgruntled looking frown, coffee stained shirt and a jacket that was just a tad too tight clearly distinguished one from the other.

"Ok, people, people, I see what's happening. You've obviously read something you didn't like. Here, let me explain."

"Explain by giving us our damn money back!" The disgruntled looking man roared.

Stan could hardly watch. Backstage he stood, hands on head, pacing around as he tried to come up with any idea for damage control. He contemplated going out to help his brother and employer but instead decided pacing around the stage like a paranoid wife being cheated would be more productive.

Some of the people in the audience looked around, lost, wondering what was going on. Whispers and grunts gathered around the room. In a matter of minutes, without Jack as much as saying another word, individuals stood up one by one, some even approaching the stage. Still, some stayed seated, scanning the room with their eyes as they speculated over what was currently taking place. They obviously had not read the article.

The complaints swarmed towards Jack. Protester by simple-minded protester congregated below him as they demanded answers and money. The volume in the room had become too loud for Jack to speak over, even with the microphone he had in hand. He looked around and then to the backstage left wing where Stan stood, pale and perturbed, motioning for his brother to get off stage. As Jack exited the stage, baffled and speechless, Laurie escaped through the same double doors she had come in through.

# CHAPTER TWELVE

That night as she sat at home alone with the fog of the day wearing off she began to think. Not about a story this time, for she knew she had one. It had pretty much been handed to her. No, this time she began to think of what had become. With Jack, with her career, with everything seemingly important in her life. Guilt overcame her. It was the strongest of her current emotions. It was not clouded by vodka or handy little pills either, for once it was tangible, unlike so many of her feelings before. She felt guilt for letting Jack fall into this. Her jealous and diseased mind slowly began to recover and realize that she was really the one to be hated. And she hated just that. Still, she sent the story.

In the office the next morning Laurie was undoubtably called into Dave's office. With an anguished face and vodka soaked breath she stumbled in. It was the first time she had ever been drunk at work. Dave, however, was far to self involved to even take notice.

"Kiddo!" He walked over and placed his hands on both sides of her face. She worried another ass slap may be soon to follow. "It's all over the place! I knew this would be big. Huge, I told ya. Its been on every local station, TV and radio."

"Well, good then." There was an unresolved tension present in her voice.

"Shit you know how many papers we've sold this morning alone? You've got requests rolling in from national stations asking you to interview Jack live. Our subscriptions are gonna be rolling in."

"Oh, Dave, he'll never go for it."

"No, no I figured, but we can figure something out. Get outta here kid, go enjoy your day. I'll fill ya in when I come up with a plan." Then, there it was, the ass slap.

Laurie walked away feeling emptier inside than she ever had. There was a void inside her, she could not quite put her finger on it, but something was missing. *Or perhaps*, she began to think, *it was never really there at all.*

– – –

Jack had by now escaped Seattle. Although less frantic than his brother, he could still feel the weight of an ominous cloud looming above. He surely wasn't used to feeling this way, always being an optimist he tended to ignore such clouds in bad times before. This time the criticism got to him though, unlike it ever had. He scanned his mind time and time again trying to come up with a way to convince himself they were wrong. Yet no luck. As he sat in the plush first class seats of the Boeing-757 aircraft he finally began to feel remorse for those he led astray. Stan rambled on in the seat next to him in a nagging voice that had now blended into the hum drum of the plane's engines. Jack was deep inside his own train of thought, lost and confused for once.

What got to him the most was not the mere disapproval, for he had always shunned most of that away. It was not the fact that his career as a self-employed guru may have come to a dramatic end either. No, what ate away at him, gnawing relentlessly, was the idea that he may be, after all, just another phony Godsend in the world today. And Lord knew, the world had plenty of them already.

– – –

Later that afternoon Laurie, while still mildly intoxicated, reached for the remote control on the arm of her plush sofa as the house phone rang. It must have been important. She let it ring one, two, three times before turning the television volume up louder to drown out the sound.

Dave Novell's voice cut through the air loudly over the answering machine, "Laurie, where the hell are ya kid?

Tried your cell. Anyhoo, get back at me, I've got big news regarding the Times. The New York Times!"

Laurie did not go for the phone or even plan to call her editor back later that day. She had about all the news she could stand and booze and tiny white pills were the only elixir for that would wash away the agony of what had become.

At around two in the morning Laurie awoke, still on her sofa in simply panties and a work shirt. Groggy, she reached for the phone trying to make out what of the last two day's events were reality. As she turned on her Einstein gadget nearby a slew of notifications flooded her screen. She widened her eyes to get a better look and pressed the button to play her messages.

An automated voice said, "Message one."

Dave's voice took over from there, "Laurie, call me, it's important."

"Message two,"

"Laurie, where the hell are you? Guess you're out celebrating. Give me a call back. It's Dave."

"Message three,"

"Laurie its Dave. Dammit kid, been trying to reach you all day. The New York Times is re-running your article. This is big. Call me now!"

As the recorded woman's voice began to mutter the phrase "message four," Laurie hung up the phone. She knew just what was reality now and a sickness overtook her. She ran to the bathroom and hunched over the toilet, resting her head on the familiar porcelain goddess.

She awoke the next morning in time to go into the office. As she swallowed a handful of aspirin and B-12 she headed out the door not quite ready to face what lay before her. Still she had not heard from Jack, nor had she really expected to.

In the office Laurie sat at her desk. She waited a moment before opening the internet browser window on her computer and typing "Jack Foster" into the search bar. The search results displayed a multitude of links to articles and blogs on Jack. Most ranting and raving in their title lines with phrases like "Jack Foster Defrauds Millions. Lawsuits to Come." Then, she noticed a link to her article on The Seattle Tribune's online paper at the top of the page. She closed the window and turned away from her computer.

Before long Dave entered the office and immediately stopped by Laurie's desk. Before he could utter a word she blurted out, "I know, I know. I got your messages. I'm thrilled." Her tone was less than enthusiastic.

He smiled at her and said, "Good. Come into my office."

She gulped and waited a matter of seconds before following him in.

Inside his office he waited for her to enter and closed the door.

"Bet you thought the Times was big news, huh? Wait for this," he said. He went to his desk, shuffled through papers, grabbed one from the stack and displayed it to Laurie. She looked at it, puzzled.

"This is gonna be your billboard! Right there outside our offices for all the highway commuters to see. What ya think, kid?"

"Well, um, Dave, it's great. It says head reporter though and I'm just..."

"The Seattle Tribune's new head reporter!" He grabbed a bottle of champagne hidden behind his desk along with two glasses. He popped the cork, filled the flutes and handed Laurie a glass as he put one arm around her lower waist. "Here ya go, kid, to success!"

*Well at least he didn't call me doll,* she thought as she took the glass from Dave.

After a near fifteen minutes of informal chatter and congratulations the two of them moved to the brown leather sofa on the other side of the office with Dave's beckoning. He reached to Laurie's far shoulder and slowly took off the cardigan draped over her to reveal a white button down.

Thoughts raced through Laurie's mind. She was all too familiar with where gestures such as this often lead to. *My God, do I do this? Should I?* Nervousness poured through her once confident mind. It was unlike Laurie to be nervous in a situation like this. Usually she would go for it but for some reason something, something unknown, was holding her back. She hated that. So she sat, frozen, allowing Dave to caress her upper arms and neck until she finally turned towards him and gave in.

There, on the couch in Dave's office, as she lay under his heavy, sweaty body Laurie tried so hard to forget the last two days and go on with her life. She wanted her sense of confidence and power back. She wanted to feel weak and confused no longer. She thought it would help. As she stood up and buttoned her shirt nearly twenty minutes later she realized it didn't.

# CHAPTER THIRTEEN

Back in Miami Jack was still in bed, comfortable as could be, as the clock struck four in the afternoon. Once again in the comfort of his own kingdom and shut off to most of the world's insanity, he had begun to have a much more optimistic outlook on his current situation.

He heard a slight *beep, beep, beep* and arose to grab his phone from his pants lying on the floor. It was an automated text message from his bank telling him his account had been updated. He clicked the link in the message leading to his online finances. The account had already begun dwindling away. Jack's account balance was now a quarter of what it was but a few weeks ago. Surely no money was coming in and prospects looked grim in the near future too, considering the recent debacle in Seattle. But, Jack was a spender. No matter how irresponsible it may have been, Jack always held true to the whole you can't take it with you sort of philosophy and his current financial situation did not phase him in the least.

Stan, on the other hand, was a saver. His nails would be bitten to the core had his savings account ever displayed a balance below six figures. Had the nuclear holocaust been well on its way, Stan would be ready. Well, as long as he could get into his bank account that is. As Stan spent the last few days pacing around his condo and at Jack's house pacing around his living room and kitchen, Jack was out enjoying what he had left.

Of course, Jack had a plan. Well, sort of. He knew there was always a way to stay on his feet. Not to mention that the materialistic items so many people sold their souls to surround themselves with were purely unimportant to Jack. So if he would have to sell his drool soaked high ticket items, so be it. Again, this too phased him not in the least.

Stan certainly could not understand what the hell Jack's problem was. Like an overbearing father, he scolded Jack almost daily. Jack could have cared less. The words stayed with him but he simply chose to live his way instead. His younger brother would constantly remind him, "I'm not going to hold your head above water, Jack. If you can't take responsibility for yourself, don't look at me." Stan did not get it. Jack had no plans of relying financially on his brother at all. For he knew how very important every single dime was to him. Still, Stan was nothing more than a nervous cat these days.

— — —

By the following week the news of Jack's so called fraud had reached nearly every corner of the country. As Laurie scoured numerous online papers, gossip and news related, she could not escape Jack's face. Interview request had poured in for him. Talk show hosts wanted him. His optimism payed off. Laurie had given up all hope of speaking to Jack and ever smoothing anything over. Jack had given up on Laurie too.

With even more money pouring into Laurie's bank account she began to realize she had little she really wanted to spend it on other than vodka and premium liquor martinis at posh little bars. She knew that Jack was happy. She could see his jovial smile in candid photographs taken of him galavanting around the Miami area. Jealous? Sure she was. But, she could barely admit that to herself among her other flaws so she drowned the very idea of such confrontation with booze and her daily medicinal cocktails.

Like Stan, Laurie was confused. Confused as to how in the hell Jack was so untroubled and she was a complete wreck.

That night her phone rang. She was sure it was Tom and she needed his affection desperately, so she reached immediately for it. DAVE NOVELL, read the screen. Dave never called her past eight O'Clock or so. A bit puzzled, she started to move her thumb towards the answer button. Realizing it was a Friday and there wasn't anything work related Dave could be calling about, she quickly summed it up to a shameless booty call and hit the ignore button twice. *If it's important he'll leave a message,* she thought. A hazy ten minutes later there was still no notification for a voicemail so Laurie assumed she was correct on her assumption in the first place. Now she really needed to forget. Nearly an hour later she was decked out in chic, revealing attire and headed out the door.

As she entered her home away from home, the bar, she saw Tom sitting at a corner, candle lit table with an intoxicatingly beautiful girl. For once, Laurie was the one intimidated as Tom caught her glance and the blonde turned around to give Laurie a condescending leer.

After sitting at the bar for what seemed like an hour to Laurie, Tom finally came over, put his arm around her upper shoulder and introduced her to his date.

"Carmen, this is my dear friend, Laurie. She's a writer for The Seattle Tribune." The girl nodded and shook Laurie's hand. "Saw that new billboard with you, congratulations on the promotion." There was no adoring doll at the end of his compliment. Laurie was taken back, especially after Tom excused himself and the gorgeous woman around his arm as they began to head out the door.

Her fragile little mind could not at the time come peacefully to terms with Tom's actions. It did not make sense to her. It was the first time in a while she had felt second best, especially with Tom. Her confidence began to falter as she became more and more jealous over the woman she only knew as Carmen. She no longer felt invincible as she obsessed over and over again about her, randomly blurting out to the bartender flaws, both existent and non, that the girl possessed.

Laurie, of course, did not have any honest feelings for Tom. Her jealousy stemmed solely from the feeling that she was no longer the most seductive girl in the bar. That she no longer had the prowess to simply snap her fingers and have boxers dropping to the floor. More so? That there was another woman she had just met who did. She hated being second string, for she had worked so hard to play first for so, so many years.

Laurie downed her martinis one after the other until the clock had struck well after last call and the bartender led her into a street-side cab. The yellow car dropped her off and she repeatedly fumbled with her key to let herself into the fancy lobby of her building. Once finally upstairs, after what felt like a hike up a rock wall, Laurie burst into tears and threw her keys across the hardwood floor.

She reached for the bottle of vodka in the freezer but grabbing it too quickly, flung it on the tile below her, thereby shattering it to pieces. Angered, she went directly to her purse and grabbed the burnt orange pill container. She emptied it into her hand putting back enough to leave three, no four pills lying in her palm. Without a whim of hesitation she gulped them down, one by one without so much as a glass of water.

"If you can't handle me at my worst you don't deserve to have me at my best," she muttered Marilyn's infamous words to a nonexistent listener as she slumped down onto her granite counter top and shortly after plummeted to the vodka and glass covered floor.

# CHAPTER FOURTEEN

It was late morning when Laurie woke up to what at the first, foggy glance appeared to be a hospital room. It was. A short and stalky nurse in kitty-cat print scrubs walked in and asked, "How are you? Had quite a night, hmm?"

"What? What is going on?" Laurie knew but still questioned the woman.

"Well, you were brought in at eight this morning. Your maid found you and called 911. Good she did too, you know how much we had to pump from your stomach? Could have killed a cow."

"Well, when do I get to go home?"

"Oh you're on suicide watch until at least Tuesday, dear."

"But I have work, I can't. I'm fine, really, I can go today."

The nurse smiled a half-hearted grin. "You just get some rest. We'll see if you feel like eating anything this evening." She left the room.

A thunderstorm of shamefulness came over Laurie. She could not believe she had ended up in the hospital and frantically she began to come up with acceptable sounding excuses in her head. It was no use. She knew nothing she could say would take away the embarrassment she was sure to feel as the scornful eyes in her world looked down upon her, as she was certain they would.

— — —

By Monday word had gotten out around the office as to the reason of Laurie's absence. She was set to be back the next week as Dave insisted she take another couple of days off after her hospital release. "I'll have Stephanie cover your stories," he said over the phone.

Surely this week's events topped the misery of the last's. Laurie drove herself deep into a self-proclaimed depression as she sat on her couch paging mindlessly through television channels and gossip magazines while thinking about just how sad her life had become. She dreaded returning to work or even going on for that matter. She blamed Jack over and over again in her mind, attempting to convince herself he brought this upon himself and her. Although Laurie was used to blaming the oh so many problems in her life on others all around her she couldn't help but feel the fingers were all pointed at her on this one.

She had tried to ease her mind with the best way she knew how, uninhibited carnality. She thought about getting up off her pity-soaked couch, freshening up and grabbing the shortest and slinkiest, yet still mildly classy dress out of the closet and making a dash for the bar. Tom had not been answering her phone calls or text messages since the last night they saw each other. Thoughts raced through her mind. *Maybe he had heard about the overdose? Would he care?* She sat there and went over the details of what she could remember of that night incessantly yet it brought no clarification.

As she tried to wrap her feeble head around Tom's disconnect she could only come up with one firm reason as to why he wanted nothing to do with her anymore. He must have heard about her trip to the hospital. After all, it is probably exactly how she would have treated a so called friend had it happened to them instead, and she knew it. To associate with someone with such problems was strictly forbidden in her fragile little world. Such a person would simply have to be tossed aside like yesterday's leftovers by conspicuous eye rolls and undying scrutiny day in and out. Her anxiety only grew as she thought about all this and her return to work in the next two days. Usually the magic little pill bottle stashed in her purse's side pocket would quell such evil thoughts, however this time Laurie did not reach for her little helpers.

Laurie's fears were not in the least misguided. The following Monday at work it seemed as though the Earth had stopped rotating for a whole 39.6 seconds as she walked into the office, thus demanding everyone's immediate attention and stares. A shy smirk came across her face as she avoided eye contact with each of her co-workers while walking past them and to her desk. Then, there was Stephanie. The one who had first introduced her to those little white bastards that got her into all this trouble. *Surely, she would understand.* With a hand placed on each hip, Stephanie caught Laurie's glance as she stood by her desk. She uttered not a word, instead raised an eyebrow like an angry teacher scolding a child for not doing their homework and shook her head before walking away. Laurie's stomach dropped to the floor. With as much desired invisibility as the freckly redhead who just transferred schools, Laurie slunk into her desk and silently begged the clock to quickly tick on to the end of the work day.

Just as four thirty came around and Laurie considered sneaking out early, her desk phone shook her as it rang loud and clear. "Laurie can I see you for a moment?" Laurie gulped and stood up to head into her editor's office. She could not even imagine what he would say to her or think about her for that matter. Part of her knew she didn't really care either.

"How are you feeling?" he asked.

"I'm fine, Dave, I just forgot how many pills I had taken. Just a little oversight, that's all."

He said nothing and slowly nodded his head. "Well, just wanted to make sure you were still up for your new position. If not Stephanie can take it for now." She could see Stephanie standing there in her mind, still shaking her head.

"No, no that's really okay, I'm fine. Really."

"Okay then," he smiled a courteous simper before returning to his work. Laurie stood there for a moment, waiting, as if he had more to say. He didn't. He peeked at her from behind his desktop computer as if to say "what?" Laurie immediately noticed the cue to exit and quickly scurried out of the office as fast as she could. She barely stopped by her desk as she grabbed her purse and flew out of the building. Just as she threw herself into her car she started to become aware of the fact that there was no one she could turn to. In fact, there was really nobody she could even call a friend.

At home Laurie poured herself her favorite concoction but again did not take the little white pill. Instead she took the rest of them from the bottle and nonchalantly emptied the entire handful into the sink's garbage disposal.

She then went back to her drink because, well, that obviously wasn't the problem at all.

She sat there and thought, without feeling pity or loathing for herself, she thought. Mostly about Jack, about what had transpired in the last month and also about their time together years ago in California. The memories shuffled through her head like photographs in an album. She saw herself, with long flowing hair smiling as she stood next to a bong with wide-framed sunglasses and a slightly stained, oversized t-shirt. A week ago she would have been disgusted with even such a remembrance of herself, but now she smiled. Jack's face came into her mind. It was gleeful all the same, only slightly younger and much more tanned. She did not know if it was Jack that made her so happy back then or if it was something else. It was hard for her to tell since she tried so eagerly to revise herself after their parting and refused to ever look back at what she once was. She sat there in silence letting the past memories and current notions pour over her and immerse her in their truth. Something pulled at her conscious, telling her she was the one to blame, both for her happiness then and her angst now.

After hours of sitting there realizing she was desperate for answers and desperate for change, she picked up her phone and dialed Jack's number. Surely she was clever enough to block the caller ID before hand in higher hopes that he would actually pick up.

It rang a third time.

"Hello?"

"Jack it's Laurie don't hang up. I'm sorry," she blurted out just before realizing she had not rehearsed anything to say to him had he answered. She only knew she wanted to ask him one thing.

The phone stayed connected.

"Look Jack, I'm sorry. I screwed up, well, a lot of things. I just need some clarification I guess."

"Okay," his voice had little emotion.

"I just wanted to know if, well, if you'd come up here. So maybe I don't know, we can talk. And I can apologize. I really need to, you don't understand how bad. And you're the only one who will underst..."

"Laurie, I can't. I'm busy. Sorry. I gotta go."

*Click.*

He certainly did not expect that. He stared at the phone as he held it in his hand before putting it back in his jean's pocket, completely perplexed at the words Laurie had just spoken. He smiled, ever so slightly.

# CHAPTER FIFTEEN

The following morning, after much nail biting and a sleepless night spent watching one too many infomercials, Laurie carried two suitcases with her down the stairs of her fancy condominium and loaded them into her SUV. She had called into work that morning right as the clock struck seven a.m., when she knew Dave would just be getting in his office. "Just give my work to Stephanie," she said right before quickly getting off the line without so much as a second thought about her decision. No plans were yet concrete for Laurie, all she had to guide her on her way now was a frozen coffee and printed out driving directions from Seattle, Washington to Miami, Florida.

A mere two days later Laurie had arrived on the outskirts of Little Cuba. Although she did not have Jack's home address she was able to find Stan's office, clearly listed on the internet. As she parked her car she took a breath and thought for a moment what on Earth she would say once she got inside. She was certain Stan would demand her to leave, cause somewhat of a scene, possibly call security and thereby bring an abrupt end to her mission. Laurie decided she would take her chances. She had come too far now.

As she entered the elevator it felt like minutes stretched out like those on a clock in a Dali masterpiece. It finally reached the twelfth floor. The door almost closed before Laurie shook herself and walked out into the tiled lobby. STAN FOSTER read the name on the glass door. She peered inside to look for any trace of a short, angry man in an Armani suit pacing around inside. Luckily, the only person in view was a twenty-something blonde receptionist who sat at the oversized front desk giggling as she browsed through countless comments on what could only be a social networking site. Relief.

Approaching the desk, Laurie smiled her business woman smile. When the girl looked up she spoke in a short, professional tone.

"Yes, I'm Laurie Dreusel," she said as she reached her hand outward. "Laurie Dreusel-Bock," she quickly corrected herself. "I did a recent expose on Mr. Foster and have been assigned another." She hoped the girl would buy it. "I'm here to meet with him and was given his home address, however getting off that exit it flew right out the window as I had it in my hand."

The girl didn't answer, but simply looked back to her computer and hit a series of keys. The anticipation Laurie felt was almost overwhelming. She wanted to pass out. Just then the girl grabbed a sheet coming out of the printer, smiled and handed it to Laurie.

"There you go, ma'am."

Laurie took the paper with an illuminated smile, grateful that there were dimwitted young girls like this prevalent in today's corporate society.

— — —

She pulled up to the address listed on the white sheet of paper. The lawn was somewhat overgrown and what appeared to be bed sheets hung from the dramatic front windows of the beige stucco home. It was a nice neighborhood, the kind trendy twenty and thirty something, single well-to-doers and unmarried couples flocked to right after the market slightly peaked. It was just where Jack fit in, sans the trendy part.

Walking up to the small, stone porch Laurie felt the familiar lump in her stomach which would usually warrant her immediate swallowing of her little white pills. Yet the pills were now gone and Laurie had only her naked self to push onward. She rang the bell. Again. Still, nobody came. She began to turn to leave just as she heard a muffled yell and swiveled around to see the pixelated figure of a man fumbling to dress himself through the thick oval glass of the front door.

A blank, dumbfounded expression came over Jack's face as he opened it to be greeted by Laurie's tragic eyes.

After a moment of silence he hugged her gently and ushered her inside.

The expected session of questions and answers played like a scene from a 1990's Tom Hanks film. Once it had been vaguely established why Laurie had come all this way and an honest apology had been made, Jack showed Laurie to his kitchen as he propped up on the counter and Laurie took a seat on the plush bar stool.

Minutes easily melted away into hours and dusk came as the two old compadres laughed and spoke of years passed. With another sip of his whiskey, Jack abruptly broke through the amicable banter with a sharp, "So what the fuck happened after you left Stanford, La?" La is what Jack and others referred to Laurie long ago, and despite her previous meetings with Jack, it was the first time she had heard that name in at least ten years.

Normally Laurie would have been offended by such a question. Well, Laurie Bock would have that is. But Laurie Dreusel was now present in the room and the unclothed woman that sat in Jack's Miami kitchen was nothing short of the incorruptible free-spirit that she once was.

"Shit, I don't know, Jack. What happens to anyone? You go in search of happiness and success and you think you find it because you're blinded by all the images you see out there, you know, of what your supposed to be." She slightly laughed, "And I still have no idea as to what the hell will make me happy. Thought I was happy. That was a joke."

Laurie did not know what exactly it was that had made her come to such a conclusion. Although the slew of calamity that had recently blown through her once seemingly perfect life offered somewhat of an answer she was still unsure as to what made her have such a change of heart. Either way, she liked the way the her unmasked self felt and was not willing to let go of her chance to finally find what she had been in search of for so long.

"Well, La, that's all I try to tell folks. You can't hang on the other guy's coat tails and hope that you will somehow be dragged down the path to triumph. You know how many saps are out there, making millions, hating what they do? Some call that success, well I don't, unless happiness is involved. You gotta be happy, La, and with that, rich or poor, you'll always find success."

She smiled as she nodded and admit-ably responded, "Guess you're not such a phony after all."

He chuckled as he clinked his glass against hers and stated, "Knew I'd get ya back," with a subtle wink.

Jack had given Laurie his bed since the spare rooms of his were littered with anything from old laptops to fitness equipment and boxed up clothes. Lying there on his sofa, Jack folded his hands behind his head and drifted right away into a sleep that could not have been more peaceful.

# CHAPTER SIXTEEN

In the morning Jack was up far before Laurie. As her weary eyes focused on Jack as she entered the kitchen and saw him standing there, she questioned, "You're up early?"

"Got a seminar today. Guess I forgot to mention. Gonna try and smooth things over. Shit, I'll even offer refunds if I have to!"

"Jack? Another seminar, I mean so soon? Are you sure that's a good idea?"

"Gotta get back in the saddle sometimes, La."

*There was that damned, never dying sense of optimism of his,* Laurie thought.

"Hope you plan on joining me?" He jokingly gestured his arm forward as if he were her escort in a fancy ballroom. "That is, if you don't plan on writing another article." He winked.

Laurie tried to smile as she nodded her head yes.

"Good!" he replied. "Then go get dressed, and hurry. We should probably get outta here before my brother pokes his nose in and starts a scene."

He tossed her a bag of popcorn that had just come out of the microwave.

"What is this?" She asked.

"Breakfast." His smile was enormous.

"Popcorn? That's not breakfast."

"What? You don't like popcorn anymore?" he joked, knowing she used to love the stuff, especially in the morning.

"No, I do, just not for breakfast. Do you have yogurt instead?" He rolled his eyes and shook his head playfully, realizing that Laurie had still not been fully reconverted. However, given the recent breakthrough of her's he smirked as he reassured himself his goal could still be accomplished.

— — —

Backstage Jack peered out at the audience. The room was starting to fill and indistinct chatter became slightly louder and louder as the moments passed. Jack could not tell if the talk was good or bad or if the faces depicted those of the same angry attendees in Seattle. A bout of nervousness came over him but he channeled it for the better, using it to plaster a smile across his face and bear that infamous jovial grin as he walked onstage.

The crowd silenced. All eyes ogled Jack, standing there in front of them. He began to speak. To his surprise the crowd remained silent. No outbursts or angry yells were heard. Jack relaxed, relieved. He apologized to any that felt wrong, asked them to reevaluate his teachings and explained to them all what he was *really* trying to say. They listened.

Standing on opposite wings backstage, both Laurie and Stan grinned in unison, Stan still unaware of Laurie's presence. A sense of solace comforted Laurie as she began to reassure herself that everything was working out. She could taste a hint of the honeyed happiness she was as of recently so badly craving. To herself, she thanked Jack. She knew no words of the matter had to be spoken either, that he somehow knew. And he did. As he glanced back at her standing on stage, glowing, he grinned. She could not help but laugh slightly as a tingling sensation came over her as she tasted the sweet joy once more. Laurie did not know where she would go from here. All she knew was that her newfound sense of peacefulness and freedom from an oh so constricting world were all she wanted from now on. Not a single thought crossed her mind as to what she would say to her editor, or for that matter, if she would even call.

Jack walked across the stage, bouncing from side to side as he pointed one by one to people in the crowd while the question and answer session took place. Still, to the entire Foster camp's relief, no bitter outcries were made. Instead the crowd was respectful and calm. *Maybe they had gotten over it already?* Laurie consoled herself with this thought as it seemed to offer her a sort of forgiveness. Stan had stopped his tense pacing and sighed in relief to himself as well.

Just then, with that perception of solace, the rear doors to the chandelier lit ballroom flew open and a man stood with what Jack immediately recognized to be a shiny handgun. It was the short, balding, disgruntled attendee from the Seattle seminar. Before most of the people seated in the rows of convention chairs could turn to see what the commotion was, two shots were fired directly at the stage. Jack ran to the left side where Laurie stood horrified as a bullet grazed his leg, thereby forcing him to the floor. The people inside ran for the exits, screaming and shrieking as two security officers raced in with guns drawn. It was too late. The man had already made a b-line for the stage and continued to fire shot after deafening shot at Jack without so much as an irate explanation. A soldier in his own right, unwavering and steadfast, he stared at Jack's body with empty eyes as he pulled the trigger again, again, again.

Laurie screamed Jack's name, begging him to crawl towards her, tears streaking her unmade face. Within seconds a S.W.A.T. team rushed in the room and ordered the man surrender as they surrounded him with a brigade of firearms. He turned briefly just before turning his gun on himself and firing one final time. His short, lumpy body fell to the floor and out spilled the little man's self-loathing and hatred for the so called injustice the world had dealt him, dripping red with what all the other radical rebels of the world might call heroism.

Laurie ran onto the stage along with Stan to assess Jack's wounds. Both of them stooped there, tear drenched, repeating Jack's name over and over again as he weaved in and out of consciousness. The paramedics arrived only moments later and whisked his body onto a stretcher after administering oxygen. Laurie and Stan darted out of the overturned ballroom after them and stared as they watched the helicopter take off with Jack in tow. Stan signaled to Laurie without so much as a single word and the both of them ran through the parking lot and took off for the hospital in Stan's car.

– – –

The night went by with surreal existence. It was undoubtably all over the news that following morning, LOCAL AUTHOR AND GURU SHOT DEAD. The words read with a pain staking shock as friends and acquaintances of Jack's picked up the various Miami papers. The television stations were covering it too, interviewing those who were at the seminar and panning back to reporters making long-faced, well rehearsed statements of sorrow about the tragedy that ensued. Laurie and Stan sat on Jack's living room couch in uninterrupted stillness as the day drifted by with a foggy, dreamlike quality that refused to allow reality to fully set in.

Three days had passed. Box by beat-up box was being carried down the stairs, through the living room and out the door by those close to Jack. Stan had wanted to begin moving any favored heirlooms or prized possessions of his brother's into his home a few blocks away. Of course, Jack had little that many others would consider valuable or even worth saving for that matter. Whether it was an old, dog-eared copy of *The Catcher in The Rye*, a stack of yellowed photographs or just a napkin with a simple little note Jack considered it special. Stan knew this and now would not dare get rid of a single item even though he once lectured his brother about saving such worthless crap.

Laurie sat in Jack's bedroom with one of the boxes she had intercepted. She had asked to see the box upon noticing a heart in red ink on the side which she immediately recognized. Inside the heart a woman's handwriting read JACK'S ROOM. They had used it to move when they decided to get an apartment together back at Stanford University. It simply amazed her that he kept the box all these years. She almost could not believe it. In bad shape, with frayed corners and a few creases and tears the box sat there pulling her into nostalgia as tiny droplets quickly filled her eyes.

What was even more surprising to Laurie was what sat inside. Photographs of the two of them scattered the box, none of them bound together or organized. She lifted out picture after picture, a few random knick-knacks she did not recognize and then a hefty stack of white, spiral bound white paper. On the top sheet of the stack large, sans-serif font read POPCORN FOR BREAKFAST by LAURIE DREUSEL. It was a novel. She had penned it back in college and it was just another part of those days she had purposely forgotten all about. Jack, however, obviously had not. She took the manuscript out and fanned through the pages, remembering how Jack would read excerpts from varying chapters, enthusiastically telling her how great it was and that she should really try to get it published. Like a blade cutting through the skin of her ribcage, something dug deep into Laurie. It was the fact that for years she had tried so painstakingly to eliminate Jack from her memory, yet he had never removed her from his.

# CHAPTER SEVENTEEN

At the funeral the next morning Laurie and Stan stood next to each other with reminiscences of younger years comforting them both. Still the two had spoken few words to one another as any further confrontation on Stan's part seemed pointless and contrite given the heavy air of the present. There, on the green cemetery lawn, over a hundred gathered to bid their final farewell to their friend.

When the ceremony came to an end Laurie lightly grabbed Stan by the arm and with a suggestion of shamefulness in her voice asked, "Stan, do you think, I mean, if it's not an issue, could I stay in Jack's place for now. Just until you figure something out."

She waited for a response, certain that even if it were a stern no that her new home was in Miami.

Stan smiled a forgiving smile, lowered his head and brought her in for a hug, "Of course you can, La. Jack would have liked that."

The two left together, with a heavy hearts but also with a feeling of renewal. After basking in the light Jack had shed on both of their lives neither could help but smile and feel the warmth he so desperately tried to radiate outward to all. In the face of tragedy the two stood tall, sure that his spirit would now carry on in them both in just the way Jack had wanted it to for such long a time.

The next morning, just as the sun was yawning in the topaz sky, Laurie pulled up to the cemetery and wandered over to Jack's newly dug grave. As she dropped her purse her phone rang a familiar, obnoxious tone. She looked at the screen to see DAVE NOVELL. Almost ignoring the call, she quickly reconsidered and pressed the green answer button. "Dave, I won't be coming in anymore," she said before he even conjured up a bellowing hello. "At all. I quit. I'm sorry. Stephanie is great for the job. She'll do great. Take care." She could hear his loud voice demanding an explanation as she removed the phone from her ear and turned it off, placing it on the dirt below her feet. She did not care to explain for she was sure he would never understand. *Just another breath wasted*, she thought, and it was now clear to her just how few breaths one may have in this world that are actually worthwhile.

She sat down on the tormented soil and silently thanked Jack, again. In lieu of flowers she brought a bag of popcorn and a can of Coca-Cola. Taking a handful out, she sprinkled a few pieces across his grave before tilting her head back and piling the rest into her mouth. It was salty and crisp and she reached into the bag once more. She let tears gently massage her cheeks as she took a few morsels and lightly buried them just under the top layer of the misplaced Earth. Every previously forbidden calorie of the butter soaked, fluffy popcorn slid down her throat as she took a swig of her long forgotten, once favorite soft drink. Then, she pulled from her bag the newly rediscovered manuscript of hers, written so many years ago, and began to read. Her dampened lips formed a faint smile. It was the best breakfast she had eaten in a very long time.

# ABOUT THE AUTHOR

Jenna Gleespen is a graduate of East Carolina University and has been a successful freelance writer since her days as a college student. Today she resides in Houston, Texas.

Aside from her work as a novelist, Jenna has had poetry of hers published in both collegiate and literary magazines and numerous articles published while working as a freelance artist.

Follow Jenna and her work at www.jennagleespen.com